BUFFALO CLOUDS

CRAIG SANDERS

This is a work of fiction. Names, characters, businesses, places, events and incidents are either the products of the author's imagination or used in a fictitious manner. Any resemblance to actual persons, living or dead, or actual events is purely coincidental.

DEDICATION

For those wonderful children:
Katie, Andrew and Paul.

ACKNOWLEDGMENTS

Books, especially first ones, don't write themselves. And so I would like to thank my fellow writers of the Capitol Hill Group of the Rocky Mountain Fiction Writers for their thoughtful criticism and support.

I would also like to thank Jerry LoFaro for permission to use his painting "Buffalo Crossing" for this book.

Finally I want to thank my wife Deborah for her encouragement, support and love.

Rain drummed on the metal roof over my head, a regular Rocky Mountain gully-washer. After turning off the shower I wiped a circle on the foggy bathroom window. Water poured across the outside glass, blurring the mountains and meadows and forests that stretched in all directions from our house.

I pressed my cheek to the window and saw the problem: another leak in the rusted downspout. It figured. The good old T Bar S Ranch was practically falling apart around our ears. Whatever wasn't worn out was leaking and whatever wasn't leaking was probably just plain broke. Patching things up had pretty much been my life for the past few years, so as I ran a towel across my chest I mentally added *fix downspout* to my chore list. Right after *find girlfriend.*

After toweling off I squinted into the mirror, hoping somehow that my wide-set eyes and shaggy brown hair had vanished down the bathtub drain and been replaced by something better, cooler.

Handsomer.

They hadn't. Neither had those ears. Maybe I just wasn't scrubbing hard enough.

Without warning the bathroom door burst open. Quickly I whipped the towel around my waist as Sam barged in, waving a path through the steamy air.

"Jesus!" I yelled. "Don't you ever knock?" School had just ended for the summer and I hadn't quite gotten used to having my kid sister underfoot every hour of the day.

She grinned and handed over a steaming mug of coffee, then whacked my rear end with a folded newspaper. "Not when I've got good news!"

"They finally found that cure for freckles?"

"Ha, ha, very funny, Cody." She tossed my jeans aside and plopped uninvited on the toilet seat. "Hilarious, okay?"

I lathered up for my weekly shave. "You know I'm a lousy mind reader, Sam. If you got good news, you best spill it."

"Actually it's great news," she said. "I got you a job!"

Please, God, not again. In the four years since Dad died Sam had taken it on herself to scour the countryside hunting up odd jobs for me. Sure, we needed the money but I didn't really need her help. Still, I guessed it made her feel useful so I usually played along. I usually lived to regret it too.

Once I finished shaving I splashed warm water on my face. "If I remember right," I said, "the last job you got for me was . . . oh, yeah, castrating cattle over at the Stevenson place."

"Got paid didn't you?"

I nodded. "A hundred bucks and all the balls I could carry. We ate Rocky Mountain Oysters for a month, remember?"

"Well, okay," she admitted. "But –"

"Let's see, let's see: what about the time before that?" I pulled a comb through my tangled hair. "Oh, right, how could I forget about fixing the Ramierez' septic tank. Talk about a mess. I stunk so bad Mom made me sleep in the barn for a week."

Sam frowned. "You know, you're awful darn picky for a guy," she said. "But this is going to make up for everything." She whipped open the newspaper and shoved it in my face: the Furnace Creek *Ingot*, our local weekly. I saw an ad circled with red marker. "Go on, check it out!"

Dad always said that arguing with Sam was like wrestling a pig in the mud; after a while it dawned on you that the pig enjoyed it. If I didn't humor her, like as not she'd be on my case all day. Sighing, I picked up the paper. The ad was small, the ink smudged, and I had to squint to make it out:

> OPEN AUDITIONS
> Speaking and non-speaking
> roles available in upcoming
> independent motion picture
> production. Experience a
> plus but not a necessity.
> Please see Ben Liebowitz by
> 3:00 p.m. Thurs., June 5.
> Room 9, Trail's End Hotel in
> Furnace Creek.

I frowned. She'd really outdone herself this time. "Come on, Sam. Look, if you're gonna try and fix me up with work, just stick to sewage and castrations, okay? Those I can handle. I mean, acting? Give me a break."

"*You* don't have to act." She snatched the paper from my hands. "And if you stop being so darn huffy, I'll –"

"And what's in it for you?"

"Me?" Like most thirteen-year-olds, Sam had an innocent little voice she trotted out whenever she wanted to get her way. I swore she practiced it every night while the rest of us were asleep. Mom always bought it, but since I was only four years older than Sam she usually knew better than to pull it on me.

"Yeah, you." I slapped aftershave on my cheeks, wincing at the burn. "You've always got an angle in there somewhere."

Sam scooped my jeans off the floor and tossed them at me. "Just you get dressed," she said, "and I'll explain it all over breakfast. I promise if you don't think it's the best thing you've ever heard I swear to God I'll never mention it again. Deal?"

As if I had a choice. "Deal."

Three stacks of half-cooked pancakes later I still hadn't decided if this was Sam's best idea, the worst, or just the out-and-out craziest. While she cleared the table I lingered over a last cup of coffee. My sister had a stubborn streak a mile wide so if I wanted to get out of the kitchen without a hassle I had to play things just right.

"Okay, let's see if I got this straight," I said in my best Reasonable Big Brother voice. "Yesterday you went to town and met this Liebowitz guy without telling me and –"

"Hey, you were busy," she interrupted. "And it's not like I went alone. I'm not completely stupid. Carrie Mondragon and her mom went too. Then Mrs. Mondragon called around a few places to check up on him. She says he's small but legit."

So much for that theory. Blanche Mondragon was the kind who'd ask the Pope for references. "Anyway," I said, "this guy is so impressed he decides to offer you and Carrie the starring roles in this movie of his."

Sam stacked the breakfast dishes loudly in the sink.

"See, there you go again," she said, glaring back over her shoulder. "You asked me to explain and when I do, you sit there making dumb jokes."

Jokes? Hell, with something like this it was all I could do to keep from laughing out loud. But rather than push any farther I took another sip of coffee and mumbled: "Sorry, Sam."

"Look, I know it's not a big part," she admitted, loading the dishwasher. "It's really not even a part at all. I'd just be an extra."

"As in 'extra gullible'?"

Sam frowned. "Be nice, Cody. See, it's a western so he needs a couple dozen of us for the crowd scenes. Walk up and down, hang around, that kind of stuff. He said he might even give some of us a line or two."

"Oh now that sounds exciting, Sam."

"It does to me. Besides, it's some pretty good money. Nearly forty bucks a day for almost a week. More if I get to talk, that is, if I have a line. Come on, it would take me a month to earn that much money babysitting."

"But you know how to babysit."

"Hey, I've had acting experience."

"When?"

"Don't you remember the 4-H Food Pageant?"

I rolled my eyes. "Sam, you were a freaking carrot, for God's sake."

"Artichoke," she shot back and slid a frying pan into

the pile of suds. "And anyone with half a brain knows green vegetables are much harder to play."

Out of the corner of my eye I noticed the kitchen clock read seven fifteen. I stood and struggled into my poncho. "Sam, I've got to get going," I said. "So cut to the part where I fit into this crazy mess."

She turned off the water. "Never thought you'd ask. Since they're going to have to build some kind of set outside town there's going to be a lot of construction work to do. Naturally I thought of you, and –"

I held up a hand; and *there* was the angle I'd been expecting. "Let me guess. You just happened to mention you have this hardworking –"

"And handsome . . ."

"Brother," I continued, "who could really, really use a job."

Sam beamed. "Exactly."

I drained my coffee and tossed her the empty mug. "Nice try," I said, "but in case you forgot I already have a job."

Her smile vanished. "Aw, you don't mean building that stupid fence, do you?"

"You got it."

"But why do you have to do that today? I mean, can't it wait? You saw the paper. He's leaving town at three."

"And San Juan Power is pumping a quarter-million volts through their new line at six. I've already lost two days on account of all the rain, Sam. It won't be your butt in a sling if that fence isn't done when the juice comes on."

Sam frowned. "That's just work. A *job* is something you get paid to do." She tapped the newspaper again. "And this one pays pretty well. Three hundred and fifty bucks a week for at least a month, maybe more. Come on, you gotta admit we could use the money."

So maybe my sister had a point. When we did the books each month, even I could see it was only a matter of time till the money ran out. Maybe not today or even next month, but probably sooner than I wanted to think about. What we really needed was a gold-plated miracle, not some crazy half-assed scheme like this. But when I told Sam how I felt she spun and launched a sponge across the kitchen that hit me square in the face.

"Jeez, what's that for?" I yelled, wiping my stinging eyes.

"What do you think?" She pounded a fist on the counter top. "That's for always acting like my big brother!"

I reached for a paper towel. "Well how am I supposed to act when you keep coming up with stuff like this? Say 'gee, good work, Sam'?"

"No, but you could at least stop being so darn protective of me, Cody! I'm not a little kid anymore. Can't you ever let me do something I want to do?"

We'd had this argument before, more often than I wanted to remember. "Not when it sounds this crazy."

"Will you stop calling it *crazy!*"

"You got a better word?"

"What about . . . 'opportunity'?"

I shook my head. "Not hardly. Face it, this whole thing sounds like nothing but a scam to me."

"That's not fair, Cody. You never even met the guy and you're already calling him some kind of con man. And just because you're afraid of something new doesn't mean I am."

My sister had developed a knack for finding all of my hot buttons. "Just shut up." I leveled my finger at her. "You've got no call to say that."

Sam shook the dripping pan at me and for a second I thought she was about to throw that too. "Oh no? I'd rather believe in something, even if it is a long shot! Y-You don't want to believe in anything anymore!"

I slammed my fist on the table. "That's enough, damn it! I'm not kidding, Sam!"

For a moment we glared at each other like a pair of coyotes circling road kill. Sam's cheeks had flushed the color of her hair and I felt warmth rise in my face too. Then as quickly as it started it was over, like the calm that follows a thunderclap.

Sam turned her back to me and stared out the window over the sink. "I shouldn't have said that, Cody," she said quietly. "It wasn't nice."

Not 'it wasn't true' or 'it wasn't right,' but under the circumstances I figured it was the best I'd get out of her.

"And I guess I'm sorry for yelling," I ventured. "It's just that I know how you are, Sam. I hate to see you wasting your time on a craz – I mean, a . . . a *thing* like this."

She dried her hands on the faded dish towel that hung from her shoulder. "And just what else do I have to waste my time on? Take a look around this place – take a *good* look – and tell me, huh?"

I had no answer, at least not one that would make sense to her, so I just grabbed my hat and headed out the door. Halfway across the porch Sam caught me by the arm.

"Look, I know I can't force you," she said. "But if you won't do it for yourself would you do it for me?"

"Do what?"

"Go see Mr. Liebowitz at the Trail's End Hotel. Today. Tell him it's okay for me to work. I'm only thirteen, remember? That means whoever's responsible for me has gotta give their permission first. Right now that means you."

Our mother had been in Chicago since last week helping care for her brother – our Uncle Lou – who'd had a major stroke at a Cubs game. He wasn't doing well so there was no telling how long she'd be gone. Although Mom left me in charge this was a little more than I wanted to deal with on my own.

"Sam, I'm not really your guardian if that's what you mean, not officially anyway. Mom's gonna have to do it."

She shook her head. "There isn't time. Liebowitz said if you'll at least give him a verbal okay Mom can sign the papers later. You know she will." She laid those big brown puppy-dog eyes on me. "So, pleeeease?"

I'd had a lot of practice saying 'no' to Sam and if only she'd started to beg and whine I would have done it in a heartbeat. But instead my kid sister just stood there dripping soapsuds on the linoleum. She didn't look like the freckled little hellcat I used to pick on whenever Mom's back was turned. And as shaky as this movie business sounded I couldn't blame her for thinking about money. I thought about it every day too. And just like that I knew I'd lost this particular argument.

"Okay, Sam," I said, tipping my battered Stetson down my forehead. "If – *if* – I have time after finishing the fence I'll take you into town, okay?"

"Absolutely!" she cried, and kissed my cheek.

I walked out into the rain, then turned and shouted over my shoulder: "And this time no macaroni and cheese for dinner!"

"It's a promise!" she yelled.

As she dashed back inside I realized it was pretty useless trying to talk her out of these crazy ideas of hers. As hard as I tried it never seemed to have much of an effect. But I guess if I was honest, no one could have talked me out of anything at thirteen, either. I had to learn the hard way.

Eventually, she would too.

So far this had been the coolest and wettest summer I could remember. After all the rain we'd had, the best way to get around was on horseback. Fortunately, that was my favorite way too. By the time Zack was saddled and ready the rain had all but stopped.

As we rode through the northern pastures, weak rays of sunlight crept between the clouds and chased themselves across the meadows of our ranch. Rain-fresh breezes washed my face. My head cleared and my heart beat a little faster, like it always did when it was just me and Zack under the awesome Colorado sky.

God, how I loved this place. The T Bar S wasn't the biggest spread in the valley, not by a long shot, but I swore it was the prettiest: nearly three square miles of forests and meadows, all tucked along the rocky banks of Tohachi Creek.

Nearby, cattle dotted the meadows like ants on a green tablecloth. There were handsome white-faced Herefords and some Angus with their glistening black coats. Beautiful to look at, but none carried the T Bar S brand. The auctioneer's hammer fell on our herd long ago. I raised the canteen to my lips and drank. Jesus, how many years had it been? Seems I could never quite remember.

In the distance a transmission tower loomed above the trees like some kind of mechanical giant who'd lost its way. Silently the rain rolled in like liquid fog and soon it seemed Zack and I were the only living things on the planet. Our breath dogged us through the chilly air and of course, water found every miserable little rip in my poncho. Soon I was soaked to the skin and feeling worse than ever.

The tower rose almost a hundred feet, its top lost in pale, gauzy clouds. A rectangle of bright green T-posts stood at attention around its base. I started the fence last week; now all that was missing were four strands of barbed wire.

I stowed Zack's saddle and tack under some bushes but as I turned him out to graze Sam's words rattled in my head, loud as bolts in a bucket: *That's just work. A job is something you get paid to do.* My kid sister was probably right though I'd die and go to hell before admitting it.

We both knew that no money would change hands over this little chore. When we signed the deal with San Juan Power the lease required us to provide the fence. Nowadays, that 'us' usually meant me.

Shivering, I pulled off my gloves and blew on my fingers to warm them. Even if Sam was right about the fence this movie business was another thing altogether. Still, I'd drive her to town like I promised. I'd give the okay for her to work too; that way she couldn't blame me when things went to hell. I hated seeing her get hurt but it was about time Sam stopped chasing dreams and got down in the muck with the rest of us.

"The fence, Cody, the fence," I reminded myself, then knelt in the wet grass and went to work.

Around noon I broke for some lunch. There hadn't been a rumble of thunder all morning so I hunkered down under an ancient cottonwood, grateful for a chance to stay dry for a while. Nearby, Zack cropped noisily on the thick meadow grass. Unlike me he didn't mind the rain.

I leaned against the rough tree trunk and chewed on the cold burrito I packed last night. Across the valley, huge cauliflower-shaped clouds boiled into the sky, promising a fresh soaking by afternoon. They were just clouds of course – I mean, what else would they be? – but today they seemed somehow . . . different. As they rose above the snow-clad mountains they caught the wind and raced toward me, rolling and tumbling like a sky full of stampeding gray beasts. At last I recognized the twisting shapes: buffalo.

Buffalo Clouds.

As I poured coffee from my thermos, something stirred in the back of my head. Buffalo. Had we really planned to raise them here on our ranch? I vaguely remembered talking about it but the memories were faded and uncertain, like a song I once knew by heart but now couldn't quite remember.

Buffalo. Bison. *Tatanka*, as the Lakota called them. Like so many things, any dreams of buffalo had died along with my father. Folding my arms, I settled back against the tree and closed my eyes. Dad wasn't coming back. The only buffalo I'd ever see were the ones circling silently overhead.

I woke suddenly to Zack's wet nose in my ear. Stretching, I glanced at my watch: one freaking fifty! I'd slept for almost two hours!

"Oh, man," I groaned and dashed back to the line of fence posts. The choice between finishing the fence and taking Sam to town was a no-brainer. On a ranch, fences always came first. But I'd given her my promise – my word – and that was one of the few things I had left that meant anything to me.

By the time I finished it was pushing two forty-five. Home was a good twenty minute ride; the drive into town at least thirty more. Maybe this Liebowitz character would stick around for a while, but that wasn't a chance I wanted to take.

"I can't believe I'm doing this," I muttered and grabbed Zack's saddle. Moments later the two of us galloped down the rocky twisting trail that led straight to Furnace Creek.

Zack's dark mane whipped back and forth in the wind and I could imagine his tail flying straight out behind him. His muscles rippled smoothly, powerfully beneath my legs and it was pretty much all I could do just to hang on.

The trail led us down through deep ravines, past scrubby willows and cottonwoods until it ended at the banks of Tohachi Creek. Usually the creek was barely a trickle but today it ran fast and cold after the rain. Cautiously I urged Zack down the slippery bank. Water foamed up around his chest in a v-shaped wave.

Halfway across he lost his footing on the rocky bottom. The saddle shifted and I tumbled headfirst over his ears and into the icy stream. Gasping, I grabbed the dangling reins and pulled myself upright. A quick tighten of the latigo and I scrambled up on his back again. We burst from the creek in a blinding spray then gained the opposite bank and galloped on toward town.

My watch read three-ten as we blew past the scattering of houses on the outskirts of Furnace Creek.

Ahead, a pack of kids huddled under the marquee of the Azatlan theater waiting for the afternoon matinee. As we galloped closer they pointed and yelled as if cheering us on.

Seconds later I reined Zack up in front of the hotel, my heart pounding against my ribs. In front of the building, old Miss Gilchrist slowly swept mud from the sidewalk into the rain-swollen gutter.

"Is Liebowitz still here?" I shouted down to her.

Without looking up she pointed a bony finger down the street. A few blocks away a white car made a right turn and disappeared behind the post office. Palmer Road – the main drag out of town – led down to the interstate in narrow snakelike curves. Our only chance was to head straight down the hillside, hoping to catch him on one of the switchbacks. Just the thought of it spooked me a little but I'd given Sam my word. At least I could try and keep it.

"YAH!" I squeezed my heels against Zack's flanks. Ducking under droopy clotheslines, we charged down the narrow alley between the hotel and liquor store. Trash cans scattered everywhere, scaring the bejesus out of half the cats in town.

We burst into the open then plunged downhill. Through the trees I caught glimpses of the car but by the time we reached the first switchback it had already passed. Without stopping we crossed the pavement and jumped the stone retaining wall, the one meant to keep you from doing exactly what I had in mind.

Zack dodged nimbly around the huge boulders littering the slope. From out of nowhere a dead tree limb ripped a hole in my poncho. Seconds later another glanced painfully off my skull and I felt something warm trickle down my face. We were gaining but the car still beat us to the next curve, so close I could smell the stink of exhaust in the air.

"Last chance, boy," I muttered in Zack's car. We managed to reach the bottom of the hill in one piece but the car sped out of the final turn, bumped across the Union Pacific tracks and vanished over a distant rise.

I reined Zack to a stop. "Shit," I muttered and climbed down from the saddle. As I kicked the dirt in frustration my knees shook so bad I could hardly stand. Mud-caked and sweaty, Zack blew and snorted at my side, jerking the reins as if disappointed the race was over. But it was. We'd tried our best and for what, a torn poncho and a gash on my head? Frustrated, I stared in the direction the car had gone and wondered how I would explain this to Sam.

A horn honked behind me. Startled, I spun and found myself facing the biggest car I'd ever seen. Fire engine red, it glistened with lots of shiny chrome trim. The California vanity plates read *59CADDY*.

The driver's door swung open and a plump, older-looking man stepped out. He wore ivory slacks and shoes, and a shirt the color of his bald, sunburned head. Smoke rose from the thick cigar clamped between his teeth. He looked me up and down like I was for sale and he had a wad of money to spend.

"Now I imagine you'd be Harrison," he said, stepping forward to shake hands. "I'm Ben Liebowitz. And you're, ah, bleeding."

His accent sounded European, German, maybe, like someone from one of those old war movies. I wiped my cheek then held out my hand in return. Though it was wet and slick with mud he shook it firmly.

"I thought you were up . . . there." I pointed down the road. "Guess I was after the wrong car, huh?"

Liebowitz nodded then pulled a folded handkerchief from his back pocket. "Nice looking horse you got there, kid." Carefully he wiped the mud off his fingers. "And that was some pretty fancy riding too."

He sounded impressed. Half the kids in the county rode as well as I did if not better, but I decided not to let on. "Uh, thanks," I said. "Comes from growing up on a ranch, I reckon."

"I *reckon*," he repeated with a broad smile, "God, I love the way you people talk." He pocketed the hankie then glanced down at the fancy-looking gold watch on his wrist. "Gotta get back to L.A. ASAP, so let's make this quick. What can you tell me?"

"Well," I began. "I'm pretty sure my Mom will let Sam work on this, this . . ." *Scam. Rip-off. Freaking waste of time.*

Liebowitz raised a thick eyebrow. "Film, kid. We call it a film."

"Right. Film," I repeated stupidly. "It's just that she's out of town for a while and —"

"Your word's good for now. You got an honest face, kid, and I'm a sucker for honest faces. I'll get the release form out in a few days. She can send 'em back when she has a chance."

Liebowitz' cigar had gone out. He struck a match and held it to the tip, puffing until his bald head was wreathed in a thick blue fog. "That sister of yours has got just the right look," he said, "so she'll do fine. But how about you? I take it she mentioned the construction we'll be doing. My contractor needs to hire a local who knows the territory."

"She did, but I'm not really interested."

"That's too bad. She talked you up quite lot the other day. Practically had me sold on you for the job." He dropped the match into a puddle where it died in a crisp sizzle. "Of course," he added, "I can understand if you're afraid of a little hard work."

I folded my arms. "Hey, I'm not afraid of any kind of work."

"Then it must be the hours," Liebowitz went on as

if talking to himself. "Fifty, maybe sixty hours a week probably sounds like slave labor, I suppose."

Obviously he'd never been on a ranch during calving season. "Heck, I've done that before," I assured him. "And then some. Plenty of times too."

He leaned against the fender. "Okay, if it's not the work or the hours would you mind telling me what it is? I'm just a little curious, you understand."

I chewed on my lip. "Look, I don't mean to be rude, but –"

"Forget rude, kid. Just be straight with me."

Straight I could handle. "See, you've got to understand that my sister's only thirteen. I mean, I love her to pieces and all, but she's not real good at telling the difference between reality and, uh . . ."

"Dreams?"

I nodded. "Something like that. She still thinks you can make anything happen if you just want it bad enough."

"And I take it you don't."

"Nope." *Not when you've been where I've been.*

"I guess I know what you mean, kid. But I suppose there are a lot worse things to believe in."

"Such as?"

Liebowitz shrugged. "Believing in nothing."

I heard Sam's mocking voice: *Just like you, Cody!*

"Look, Mr. Liebowitz," I said as I climbed back into

the saddle. "It's late and I'm beat. Sam wants to work for you. I don't. Now is there anything else we need to talk about?"

"Not a thing, kid. You go tell little sis I'll have a shooting script out to her in a few days. With her voice, I'm planning on giving her a few lines with Billy."

Billy? I looked up. "Billy who?"

"She didn't tell you?" Liebowitz opened the driver's side door. "He's the one this whole picture's about. Young man about your age. Lived right around here over a hundred years ago: William Tobias MacAllister."

My jaw dropped. "Wait, you don't mean Billy MacAllister, do you?" I asked. "The boy who drove cattle up here from Santa Fe?"

He nodded. "One and the same. Know about him?"

Did I ever! When I first heard his story I was just a kid, snuggled in bed while night winds howled outside my room. I remembered the cinnamon-sweet aroma of hot chocolate and the warmth of my soft thick quilt. Best of all, the sound of Dad's deep voice as he sat on my bed spinning stories about young Billy MacAllister.

"Hey, are you all right?" Liebowitz had paused halfway inside the car. "You look like you just saw a ghost."

I shook my head, feeling momentarily disoriented. "Ah, you're probably not going to believe this," I said. "But we're related."

Liebowitz settled onto the seat. "That's funny," he said and raised an eyebrow. "You sure don't look Jewish."

I had to laugh. "Not me and you. Me and Billy."

"Oh sure you are." He teased the wrapper off a fresh cigar. "And Wyatt Earp is my ex-brother in law."

"No, I swear to God," I said, feeling a sudden flush of excitement. "Come on, you know the story; Billy's folks settled near here in the 1860s. My family – the Harrisons – arrived a few years later. Then my great-great grandfather married Billy's younger sister or something like that. The way I figure it makes us sort of cousins or something. About twenty times removed, that is."

Liebowitz leveled a finger at me. "Kid, if you're making this up just to impress me . . ."

"I swear I'm not," I said, stroking Zack's neck. "In a place as small as Furnace Creek just about everyone's related in some way or another."

A huge grin spread across his face. "Well, I'll be damned," he said and slapped his hand on the steering wheel. "I'll be God-double-damned! And that being the case it hardly seems right you not taking the job, seeing as you're related. Who knows, maybe having you and little sis on the payroll might bring me a little luck. God knows I could use it."

I felt myself weakening, almost as if my long-forgotten cousin Billy was standing beside me, whispering encouragement in my ear.

Liebowitz turned the ignition key and the Caddy's big V-8 roared to life. "Look, kid," he said. "This isn't exactly rocket science we're talking here, just basic carpentry. If you can swing a hammer without mashing a thumb you'll do fine. Three-fifty a week and you get paid every Monday. If it don't work out we part company with no hard feelings, *capiche?*"

"Uh, I reckon maybe I could give it a . . . try," I said at last.

I didn't think his grin could stretch any wider but it did. "Then I *reckon* I'll be in touch," he said. Tires screeching, he swung the car out onto Palmer Road and sped out of sight.

God, what had I gotten myself into this time? As I turned Zack toward home the sun crept from behind crimson-edged clouds. Wisps of steam rose from the wet pavement and hung motionless in the humid air, mysterious and silent as ghosts.

When I awoke the next morning I wondered if I'd made a mistake. By the end of the week I was sure of it. Every time I blinked, Sam was calling me to the phone to talk to Liebowitz. Little stuff mostly, some errands and a lot of phone calls, but it added up. It was starting to piss me off too. I still had chores to do and it griped me that I wasn't getting paid for this extra running around. Finally he called with 'one last favor' to ask. I was busy changing the brakes on our old pickup, so I took the call out in the garage.

"Bad news," he said. "J.T. tells me he may have, uh, overstated his riding abilities."

"Whoa, back up a minute. Who's this J.T.?"

"Jason Travis Kelley," snapped Liebowitz, spitting out the words like they tasted bad. "J.T. to his friends, what precious few he has. He's playing Billy MacAllister. Didn't I tell you about him?"

"No, you didn't. But do you mean he lied about being able to ride a horse?"

Liebowitz cleared his throat. "Lie's a little harsh, kid. Between you and me, let's just say he might have exaggerated a bit."

"Uh-huh. And what do you mean by a 'bit'?"

"Probably a few more hours' practice. Sort of a refresher course."

Why was he telling me this? "All right, so you got yourself a kid who needs some riding lessons," I said. "What's it got to do with me?"

He cleared his throat. "I was hoping that you could do it."

I nearly dropped the phone. "Me? But I'm not a riding instructor."

"Listen, kid," he said. "Last week I saw you and that horse of yours tear almost straight down a hill at damn near a full gallop. Now maybe you do that kind of stuff every day but it impressed the hell out of me, that's for sure. Come on, giving a few lessons ought to be a piece of cake."

"Maybe," I said. "But aren't there about a thousand places he could get lessons there in Los Angeles?"

"Sure there are but that's not why I'm asking. See, J.T. just turned fifteen. He has a little problem, uh, relating to adults. Hell, sometimes I think he has a problem just talking to adults."

"So?"

"So, I think he'd learn better from someone nearer his own age. Especially someone who rides like you do. We're starting to film down in New Mexico next week so I'd just send him out a few days early."

I fished the greasy lug nuts from my pocket. Nothing like a compliment, especially one so prettily wrapped in bullshit. I threaded a nut on each lug and spun them home. Decisions like this always made my head hurt.

"Look, I've really got to be honest with you Mr. Liebowitz —"

"Ben. Please call me Ben."

Good old Ben Liebowitz seemed about as slippery as an otter but just for grins I decided to play along. "Okay, Ben," I said. "For starters, I swear I spent half of last week running around town doing errands for you."

"Said thanks, didn't I?"

"Sure, but like we say around here, gratitude's fine but it don't buy the beans."

"'It don't buy the beans,'" he repeated. "Hmm. That's a great line, kid. Real authentic-sounding too. Maybe we can even work it into the script."

"Yeah, and I'd be honored, okay? But all this stuff is way more than I bargained for. I thought you just wanted a laborer."

"And there'll be plenty of time for that," said Liebowitz, "but right now this is more important. If J.T. can't ride there won't even be a picture, so this has to come first. But I guess you know your limitations better than I do, kid. I don't want you in over your head. If you don't think you can handle it then just say so."

"Now just hold on a minute," I said. "That isn't it at all. What I mean is that I'm not doing anything else for you without getting paid for it."

"Problem solved. As of five o'clock today you are on the payroll. Three fifty a week, as promised."

He agreed so fast that I hadn't left myself an out. "Okay," I said grudgingly. "Then I guess you got yourself a deal. But what's so special about five o'clock?"

"Uh, because that's when his bus arrives."

I glanced down at my watch and dropped the tire iron. It clattered loudly on the concrete floor. "Did you say five? B-but it's almost —"

"Four-thirty, mountain time. Guess you'd better get a move on, huh?"

"Jesus," I stammered, "You might have given me a little warning!"

"I know, I know, but it's been hell trying to put something like this together. I guess time just got away from me."

"But what if I'd told you no?"

"Oh, you seem pretty bright," he replied. "I figured

you'd bite if I gave you a chance so I stuck J.T. on the Greyhound yesterday morning. When he gets there, give him a little test ride to see what he can do. I'll call tonight for a report. Be sure to have one."

The Mexicans had a word for what it took to play a hunch like that: *cojones*.

After a couple of quick phone calls I dropped the truck down off the jacks. But when I backed out of the garage Sam dashed onto the porch with a food-splattered apron tied around her waist.

"And just where do you think you're going?" she shouted through cupped hands. "Dinner's almost ready!"

I leaned out the window. "To town," I shouted. "I've got to meet J.T. at the bus stop in thirty minutes."

"Who's J.T.?"

"He's Billy!"

A puzzled look crossed her face. "Billy? I thought you said he was J.T."

"No, J.T. is Billy. That is, he's *playing* Billy – I mean, oh hell, just get in. I'll explain on the way."

Sam dashed back into the house and a moment later plopped down beside me holding a can of pop in each hand. "What about dinner?"

"It'll keep." As I punched the gas I had a sinking feeling in the pit of my stomach; this was going to be a very long afternoon.

Sam listened while I filled in the details then whistled

softly. "Hoo-eee. Man, talk about some major nerve."

"Tell me about it. But what really gripes my butt is that he just assumed I'd say yes when he stuck this kid on the bus." I glanced over at my sister. "Be honest; am I really that big a pushover?"

Sam popped the top on her can and handed me the other one. "Usually." She slurped the foam that bubbled out. "But God, wouldn't it have been totally funny if you'd told him to stick it?" She giggled. "And I can hear him too. 'Whaddya mean no, kid? I really need yer help here, kid'."

We both laughed. Leave it to Sam to make me smile. My sister took another long sip and wiped a hand across her mouth. "By the way, you don't happen to know what this J.T. character looks like, do you?"

"Not a freaking clue. Liebowitz said he just turned fifteen but that's about it. But don't worry, I have a hunch he's gonna be pretty easy to spot."

By the time we hit Route 550, Sam had settled into the seat with her sneakers propped on the dash. She pulled a bunch of papers from her back pocket. I recognized her dog-eared copy of the film's shooting script. It arrived a few days ago and she'd hardly put it down since.

"You know, this thing is really great, Cody." She tapped the pages. "Seriously. You ought to read it."

Goose bumps prickled my arms; I knew the story all

too well. Nearly a hundred and fifty years ago, fifteen-year-old Billy MacAllister rode north with his father and uncles, driving cattle to the newly-founded town of Furnace Creek.

As a kid I'd heard it so often I could practically recite it from memory. But last night after I climbed into bed I dreamed about it too. There was a young cowboy – it had to be Billy – and three men riding across rolling, sagebrush-covered hills with a herd of scraggly longhorns. The boy rode point while the other men followed behind in the dust. Overhead, the sun was bright and hot and I watched them wipe the sweat and dust from their faces. That was it – nothing but endless riding under a blazing sky. It was so vivid, so real that it left me feeling just a little spooked. I mean, it was bad enough that Billy had 'talked' me into working for Liebowitz; was he going to take over my sleeping hours too?

Casually I glanced at Sam. "Do you ever remember your dreams?"

She looked over and brushed some windswept hair away from her eyes. "Why?"

"I don't know; I was just curious."

Sam shrugged. "Sometimes, I guess, but only if it's a totally cool one. Like when I made the cover of *People* magazine. See, I was leaning against a Porsche in front of my new condo in Aspen. The article was about the Twenty Five Most Beautiful People of the Year."

"I think I get the picture," I said slowly.

"Oh, and you were my gardener."

"Hey, I said dreams, not nightmares."

She shot me a grin. "Rule number one; don't ask a question if you can't take the answer."

I hung my arm out the window. Served me right for asking. Next time I'd keep my stupid dreams to myself.

With tourist season underway the traffic was terrible; it seemed like half the country had decided to visit Colorado this week. A huge RV with Ohio plates wallowed past in the left lane then swung in and cut me off. I leaned on the horn while the driver and I exchanged one-finger greetings. On top of that there was a lot of road construction to deal with. We made such lousy time it was nearly five-thirty when we reached the bus stop in town. Except for a teenager leaning against the side of Ortiz Drug, the brick-paved street was deserted.

Sam pointed. "You think that's him?"

"Could be." The kid looked a good half-foot shorter than my five-ten and not much taller than Sam. But his clothes were a dead giveaway; skinny black jeans stuffed into orange high top Nikes, mirrored sunglasses and a purple Lakers cap – backward, of course. Nobody in Furnace Creek dressed like that.

Finally he noticed us gawking through the windshield and shuffled over as we got out. "You Harrison?" he asked warily.

"Cody." I held out my hand. "Hey, I'm really sorry we're late getting here but –"

"I damn well hope you are," he said, ignoring my outstretched hand. "First I get to spend a day and a half on a stupid bus – a *bus* for Christ's sake – then I gotta stand around in this pissant little town waiting for you!"

Tired and dirty, I was in no mood to be hassled by some kid I'd just met. Besides, this was *my* pissant little town too. "Ease up," I said. "Liebowitz didn't even tell me you were coming till an hour ago, so don't dump on me."

He shook his head. "I should have known. That's about how much time he gave me before he shoved me on the bus. I hate the way he does things, but that's Ben. Better get used to it." That said he offered his hand and grudgingly I shook it. "Anyway, I'm J.T. Didn't mean to bark at you, man. No hard feelings, okay?"

Then he pushed the sunglasses up onto his forehead and gave Sam a huge grin. "And who's our babe, here?"

Sam giggled but I didn't see what was so funny. After that half-assed apology, J.T. Kelly struck me as a sawed-off jerk. "Our babe," I replied, "is Samantha. My sister."

"Oh. Well, nice to meet you," he said with exaggerated politeness.

Sam pumped his outstretched hand. "My friends all call me Sam." She shot me a look that screamed *'stop embarrassing me!'* "And welcome to beautiful downtown

Furnace Creek."

J.T. glanced down Ute Avenue, finally noticing the old dog scratching itself in the middle of the street. "Wow," he said. "Looks exactly like I thought it would."

I liked him less with every passing second.

Yawning, he gave us a view of perfect white teeth. "I'm really beat." He jerked his thumb toward some expensive-looking aluminum suitcases sitting on the sidewalk. "Would you two mind getting those for me?"

While J.T. climbed into the truck Sam and I fetched his gear. "What a little jerkoff," I muttered.

She looked up to see if he was listening. "Maybe," she said. "But I think he's totally cute."

I tossed the cases into the bed of the truck. "Cute or not, if he tries to tip me for carrying his bags I think I'm gonna whomp him."

As we headed out of town the two of them jabbered away like a couple of magpies. So far I didn't much care for J.T. Kelley but I envied the way he struck up a conversation with a girl he'd just met. I could never seem to do that no matter how hard I tried.

Ten minutes later we reached the parking lot of the Ayo-Kay Corral. "Aw, come on, Harrison," J.T. said, his voice just below a whine. "Can't this wait till tomorrow?"

Sam nodded. "Yeah, Cody. What'll it hurt?"

My patience was running thin. "Look you guys, Liebowitz wants a progress report tonight and I've gotta have something to tell him." I turned off the truck and pocketed the keys. "Besides," I said to J.T., "this'll just take a few minutes and then I can drop you off at the hotel, okay?"

He opened his mouth but must have realized he didn't have a whole lot to say in the matter. Head down, he followed us across the parking lot.

Sam caught up to me and tugged my elbow. "Cody, what horse did you line up for him?"

"I told Mr. Pritchett I needed to rent Ginger for a couple of days."

She breathed a sigh of relief. "Good choice. She's a total sweetheart. He ought to be able to handle her."

Sam climbed atop the arena fence while I led J.T. out to where Ginger waited for us. She was a little skittish sometimes but otherwise a real doll, gentle and well mannered. She wouldn't have been the best choice for a new rider but she'd do fine for someone who already knew the basics.

Friendly as usual, she lowered her head so I could scratch behind her ears. I nodded toward a saddle and blanket draped over the fence. "Saddle her up," I told him, "then just give me a few turns around the arena so I can see how well you sit a horse."

J.T. stared at me like I was speaking Chinese. "Ah, you do know how to saddle a horse, don't you?" I asked.

"Of course." He jammed his hands deep in his

pockets and kicked the dirt. "But would you mind this time? Like I said, I'm really beat."

Like I'm not? Biting my tongue, I saddled Ginger and adjusted the stirrups. "Here." I said and handed him the reins. "Or do you want me to ride her for you too?"

He took a deep breath then planted a foot in the left stirrup. Grunting like a mule he grabbed the pommel and hauled himself onto Ginger's back, overbalanced and nearly fell out of the saddle. The mare's ears shot straight up and she danced nervously from side to side. I was about to tell him to hold up a minute when J.T. snapped the reins against Ginger's neck, dug in his heels and bellowed: "GIDDY-YAP!"

Mild-mannered Ginger leaped like she'd been smacked with a two-by-four. Snorting furiously she charged across the arena as if wolves were on her tail. J.T. stood bolt upright in the stirrups, flapping his elbows like some kind of wounded bird.

Sam jumped down from the fence and we lit off after them. "The reins," I shouted, "use the goddam reins!"

Once Ginger reached the end of the arena she whirled and raced back toward us. As Sam and I scattered, J.T. apparently decided he'd had about enough fun for one day. He dropped the reins then threw one leg over the saddle and jumped. His left foot caught me square in the shoulder, spun me around and drove me face first in the mud. Then he landed on my back and knocked the wind out of me.

A moment later Sam appeared holding his battered Lakers cap. Once she saw I wasn't dead she reached down helped J.T. to his feet.

"Well," she said with a laugh, "at least you picked a soft spot to land. But seriously, would you mind telling me just how many times you've ridden a horse?"

J.T. replaced his cap. "Uh once," he said. "Not bad for my first time, huh?"

On the way back to the hotel Sam sat quietly between us while he pretended to sleep and I pretended I didn't want to pound the crap out of him. What a freaking little liar he turned out to be and now I was the one stuck with him! This was *way* more than I bargained for. I wondered what I could possibly do about it but my mind was a complete blank.

At last we dropped him and his mirrored sunglasses and aluminum suitcases on the front stoop of the Trail's End Hotel. "Don't suppose they have Wi-Fi?" he asked as he climbed down from the truck.

"I got you a room," I said, ignoring his question. "It's not fancy but it's clean. Miss Gilchirst can probably rustle you up a sandwich if you're hungry. Otherwise, get some sleep and have your butt out here by seven tomorrow morning. And wear something you don't mind getting dirty."

He disappeared inside without looking back.

"A few hours' practice, my ass," I muttered, staring after him. "Hell, he acted like he hadn't even seen a damn horse before today."

"Oh come on. He didn't do all that bad, Cody."

Was she even watching? Grinding the gears, I made a U-turn and headed home. "Easy for you to say," I growled. "You'd see it differently if the little butt-wipe had landed on you."

She laughed. "Okay, you got me there. But seriously I'm surprised he even tried to ride her."

"Sam, what the heck are you talking about?"

"If you hadn't been so busy acting all pissed off you might have noticed," she said. "The poor guy was practically scared to death."

That made no sense. "Of what, for Christ's sake?"

"Of Ginger, stupid. Oh sure, he talks big, but all that attitude was just his way of hiding how frightened he was. Trust me on this one."

While I'd never met someone who was actually afraid of horses I got a sinking feeling Sam might be on to something. Although I hadn't given it much thought at the time, J.T. always managed to keep me between him and Ginger. What's more, he hadn't even bothered getting acquainted with her either. I'd been taught never to try and mount a strange horse without taking time to say 'howdy'.

My head spun. I should have known it sounded too

easy over the phone. "Great. What am I going to do now?"

She held up her hands. "I love you, Cody," she said, grinning. "But I'm afraid you're on your own with this one."

Next morning I stood at the kitchen window and sipped coffee as fat raindrops hammered the glass. I hadn't slept worth a damn. My back still hurt from breaking J.T.'s fall, but that wasn't it; I had Ben Liebowitz on the brain. Last night he called just as we got back from the Ayo-Kay.

"Sounds like you got yourself a little problem there, kid," he said after I filled him in.

"Me? But he's your star."

"And your responsibility. We have a deal, remember? You're the one who said you could teach him, not me."

The longer we talked the more I suspected he knew about J.T.'s fears all along. He was probably going to dump the kid on some unsuspecting trainer when I wandered into the picture, wide-eyed and innocent as a newborn calf. Finally I wrangled four more days of training, but I tossed and turned all night with Ben's last words buzzing in my ears: *It's all up to you now, kid.*

"Cody, do you want peanut butter or lunch meat on your sandwich?" Sam asked as she stood at the kitchen table, making a couple of sack lunches for J.T. and me.

I moped over and helped myself to a slice of bread. "What I really want is some advice."

Sam grinned. "Sorry, fresh out. Let's see, how about a nice PB&J for the big movie star and some pickle loaf for the riding instructor?"

I made a face. "You know I hate pickle loaf."

"And *you* know I hate listening to you whine." She spread a layer of peanut butter across a slice of bread then buried it under a blanket of grape jelly. "That's all you've done since J.T. got here, Cody. I swear it's driving me nuts." She slapped the sandwich together and started on another – peanut butter, to my relief. "So exactly what are you planning to do with him today?"

"I don't know. When he falls off I'll just keep putting him back in the saddle till he figures it out. Maybe if I can find some duct tape . . ."

Sam shook her head. "Be sure and let me know how that works out for you," she said. "Look, we both know teaching J.T. is going to be a total pain. You saw what he's like; he can't even get near a horse without almost peeing his pants. But that's tough; he's here and he needs your help. So use your head and find a way to give it to him."

Clearly I'd get nothing helpful out of Sam. "Terrific," I said, feeling the first throb of a headache. "But who's going to help me?"

At the hotel I found J.T. on the front bench, drinking coffee out of a Styrofoam cup. Besides a Hard Rock Cafe t-shirt, old jeans and boots, he wore a bright yellow poncho tied around his slender waist. He hadn't lost the Lakers cap. Or his cheerful attitude for that matter.

"That place is a total pit," he muttered, climbing into the truck. "I asked for an early call so the old lady hands me an alarm clock and says to wake myself up."

That sounded like Miss Gilchrist. "Oh, and the Wi-Fi . . .?"

"Nada. No bars on my cell phone, either." He scrunched down in the seat. "Hell, the place is so old it's lucky to have indoor plumbing."

As we drove through town, J.T. stared at the brick buildings along Ute Avenue. "Hey, Harrison," he said, "Isn't this supposed to be some kind of ghost town?"

"Not this part. Old Furnace Creek — the original town site — is up there somewhere." I nodded toward the rain-shrouded mountains. "But after the railroad came through they all moved down here and started over."

"Lot of good it did 'em," he muttered.

We reached the Ayo-Kay in a steady drizzle that

looked like it wouldn't let up anytime soon. A few forlorn-looking ponies stood under a shed, saddled and ready just in case some tourists might stop by for a ride. As we walked among the horses J.T. got all shaky and nervous again, just as Sam predicted. At last I led him down a narrow corridor between the office and tack room and into the stables.

He clapped a hand across his nose. "Damn!" he said through his fingers. "What stinks in here?"

"Don't worry, you'll get used to it."

"Why? We're going out to ride, aren't we?"

I shook my head. "Not in this weather. Till the rain stops we're going to stick around here and clean stalls."

"What, you expect me to . . . to shovel shit?"

Oh brother. "Around here we call it mucking but yeah, that's the plan."

He snorted. "Get real, Harrison. I'd rather be out in the freaking rain."

"Not me. Besides, Mr. Pritchett and I made a deal. He won't charge for the horse rental if we clean stalls. Fair trade all around."

"That's bullshit," he snapped.

"Technically it's horse shit."

"Not funny." J.T. crossed his arms. "Come on, I know what Ben told you; you're supposed to teach me to ride, not make me do your damn chores," he said. "So forget your deal. I'm not wasting my time cleaning up this place!"

Yesterday I would have wanted to pop him one but maybe Sam had given me some things to think about after all. "Gotta tell you," I said, hands on my hips, "Good old Ben isn't too happy with you right now. In fact, last night he was real interested in what I told him about your riding skills."

Uncertainty flickered across his face. Staring at the ground he dragged the toe of his boot in the dirt. "So you ratted me out, huh?"

"I just told him what I saw."

"Was he pissed?"

"Does he usually yell and swear?"

"No."

"Then trust me, he was pissed. But don't take my word for it; maybe you should call him yourself." I nodded over my shoulder. "There's a phone in the office there. I'm sure he'd love to tell you personally."

J.T. shook his head. "I'll pass."

"Suit yourself. Anyway, ol' Ben gave me four days to teach you how to ride. He said something like 'do whatever you want as long as it doesn't leave a mark'."

He sighed. "That's Ben. The man's all heart."

"So, you want to get started?"

"Okay, okay." He held up his hands. "You win."

Hands shoved in his pockets, he grumbled along behind me. When we reached the last stall I handed him a pitch fork and unlocked the gate. One look inside and he backed away with the handle clutched to his chest. "Damn it, Harrison," he said, voice rising, "there's a horse in here!"

"So what? You're going to muck the stalls, not redecorate them. Don't worry, you're not going to get stepped on."

"How do you know?" he shot back. Throughout the stable, horses whinnied and craned their necks to see what all the ruckus was about.

"Okay, so I know they're big," I said. "But a horse will go out of its way to avoid stepping on you if you give it half a chance. Just let them know you're there so they don't get all spooked. If you're nervous you could try, uh, talking to them."

"Yeah?" J.T. looked puzzled. "About what?"

I smiled. "Well, it's going to be a pretty one-sided conversation, so I guess it doesn't really matter. See, it's not what you say that calms them, it's the sound of your voice."

His face reddened. "I knew that. It's not like I'm totally stupid, Harrison."

"Didn't say you were. Oh, and don't be afraid of touching them either. You know, pat their necks. Scratch their backs. These horses love attention. Just don't startle them or you're liable to get a hoof up your butt." I handed him some work gloves. "Toss the dirty straw and manure out of each stall and pile it up outside the gate. We'll clean that up later when we put down fresh bedding."

Reluctantly he pulled on the gloves. "And where are you going to be? Just in case, that is."

"Right over there in the next row." Gently I pushed him into the stall and closed the gate. "Get busy, okay?"

Starlight was plump and lazy, probably the best-natured pony in the string, but you never know how a horse will react to someone new. Since Liebowitz probably wanted his star back in one piece I kept a close watch through the gaps in the wall boards. Slowly, J.T. worked around the stall, his eyes glued to the horse. He pitched the manure and straw over the gate, breathing like he'd finished a marathon. Poor Starlight just stared, probably wondering what she'd done to upset him.

"Hey J.T.," I called out. "I can't hear you!"

"What?"

"Remember what I said about talking to them?"

"Oh, right." He cleared his throat. "N-Now don't you mess with me, horse. I've got one mean son of a bitch for a lawyer and I'm not afraid to use him."

Maybe it was just as well Starlight couldn't understand him. "Keep that up," I shouted and went back to work, wondering if this or anything would help.

Rain dribbled through chinks in the roof as we mucked our way toward the opposite ends of the stable.

Horses whickered softly. In the rafters, Lizzie the stable cat kept watch on us, a shadow with sunset eyes. I strained to hear J.T.'s voice. Crazy as it seemed, he was singing; an oldie, but one of Dad's favorites and one I knew by heart.

"There is a house in New Orleans, they call the Rising Sun. And it's been the ruin of many a poor boy, and God, I know, I'm one."

I listened for a while then joined in loud and off-key on the last verse:

". . . I'm heading back to New Orleans. My race is almost run. Going back to end my life, beneath the Rising Sun."

I glanced over the gate. From the other end of the row, J.T. leaned out of a stall, grinning from ear to ear. And so the two of us spent the rest of that rainy morning in the stable, as J.T. put it, just singing and shoveling shit.

We ate lunch in the office. Despite a promising start things weren't moving along quite as fast as I hoped they would. Maybe I needed to try something just a little bit more hands-on.

"Now what?" he asked as I led him back into the stable. "It's stopped raining. I thought we were finished in here."

At least he hadn't complained about the smell. "We're done mucking all right," I said as we stepped back into a stall. "Now comes the fun stuff."

I slipped a bridle over the horse's ears then handed the leader to J.T. The way he cringed you'd think I'd offered him the business end of a rattlesnake. I grabbed his hand and folded his fingers around the worn nylon strap.

"Just follow me and she'll follow you," I told him then set off down the row of stalls, reassured by the *clip-clop-clip-clop* as J.T. and the horse plodded along behind me.

Outside I picked up a curry comb. "Okay, welcome to Grooming 101. Just watch me for a minute then you get to do it." I started working on the mare's back. Fine brown dust filled the air as I coaxed muddy flecks from her coat. She closed her eyes and you could almost hear her sigh with pleasure.

J.T. smiled. "Wow, she really likes that, doesn't she?"

"Loves it, you mean." I handed him the comb. "Here, you give it a try."

Tentatively he ran the comb across her coat but then jumped back as her skin twitched beneath his touch. "What happened? I-I didn't hurt her, did I?"

"Nope. She's just saying 'oh baby, that feels *so* good'. Keep at it and don't be afraid to bear down a little harder. Work your way around her back then down her sides and legs. And remember to –"

"Keep talking. I won't forget."

Walking away, I sat on some hay bales to watch. As he worked with the comb, J.T. spoke in a gentle voice, apparently forgetting I was in earshot. "How far do you reckon it is back to Furnace Creek, Pa?" he said. "How long will it take to get there with the cattle and all?"

I recognized the words: J.T was practicing his lines for the movie. Frowning, I tipped my hat over my eyes and leaned back against the hitching rail. Christ, would I ever be free of Billy MacAllister? Last night before bed I tried my best to put that story clean out of my head. But trying not to dream about something pretty much guarantees you will. Sure enough, the night was filled with cowboys and cattle. Only this time I wasn't just watching the action, I was a part of it; three men and me, alone on a dusty trail with a herd of longhorns. It was so real that when I woke up the next morning I swore I felt grit crunch between my teeth.

Something nudged my boot. "Hey, no fair sleeping on the job, Harrison."

I opened one eye. J.T. stood proudly by the horse's side. "Well, what do you think?" He rested his hand on her back like he'd been around horses all his life. "Not bad, huh?"

The mare's coat shone like a first place winner at the State Fair. Yawning, I stood and stretched. "Nice," I said. "That's really good. You sure you've never done this before?"

J.T. grinned. "Just to my dog." He stroked the mare's neck then scratched behind her ears when she lowered her head for him. "I've never seen anything, er, anybody

. . . I mean, a horse this beautiful," he said. "Does she have a name?"

"Sure: Ginger."

"From yesterday? No way!"

I nodded. "Surprising, huh? After what happened I thought you two would never forget the sight of each other."

"Guess I just didn't recognize her standing still." He stroked her muzzle. "Sorry about last night, girl." Ginger gave him a friendly shove with her nose and he laughed.

All at once I saw the opening I'd been hoping for. "You'll find she's very forgiving," I said. "And after a first-class grooming job like that I'm sure she wouldn't mind if you sat on her back for a while."

"But she isn't saddled."

"You don't need one just to get acquainted. So come on." I took a knee and locked my fingers to give him a leg up. "If you really want to, that is."

A determined look crossed J.T.'s face. He rested a foot in my cupped hands and I boosted him up and on to Ginger's back. He settled gently into place, neat as a cat.

"Oh, man," he cried. "Man, this is totally *awesome!*" Arms out, he looked down on me, grinning like a kid on Christmas Day. "It feels like I'm ten feet tall! Why didn't you tell me it was this cool, Harrison?"

"Because I couldn't," I said. "It's just one of those things you have to find out for yourself."

We spent the rest of the drizzly afternoon in our ponchos, out in the muddy arena grounds. While Mr. Pritchett watched from the office window I led Ginger around by the halter, back and forth, round and round, getting J.T. accustomed to the feel of her rolling gait. He seemed to be actually enjoying himself; maybe there was hope after all.

About six-thirty I dropped him off at the hotel. "Same time tomorrow morning?" he asked, getting out of the truck.

I nodded. "Don't forget to wind your alarm clock."

"I won't. But do we still have to . . ." He made an exaggerated shoveling motion with his arms.

"Yeah, but only for the next three days."

Grinning, he flipped me a good-natured finger and swaggered away, whistling *The House of the Rising Sun*. At the door he gave me a brief wave before disappearing inside. As I headed for home I breathed a sigh of relief; he seemed to be turning into a cowboy right before my eyes.

After a promising start, by noon the next day things had gone to pieces again. I had spent the whole morning teaching J.T. all the tools of basic horsemanship: how to mount; how to sit; rein-handling techniques, everything I learned when I was a kid. At first it seemed to come easy to him. J.T. had a lean athletic body and sitting up there in the saddle he looked relaxed and confident. But when I turned the two of them loose nothing went right. If he wanted her to stop she took off running. If he called for a trot she broke into a canter. And no matter which way J.T. wanted to go Ginger insisted on the opposite direction. It would have been funny if I didn't have a deadline to meet.

A door opened and Mr. Pritchett stepped out of his office. Seeing me, he fired up a cigarette and ambled on over. Lowell Pritchett had been Dad's best friend and I'd known him since I could remember knowing anyone. Nearly sixty, he always spoke his mind so I braced myself for some harsh comments on my teaching ability. To my surprise he just said, "So how's things gettin' along there, Cody?"

Like he didn't have a pair of eyes. "What do you think?" I muttered. "I just can't seem to figure out what's wrong. I taught him everything as best I could and, well, just look at him." I glanced at the older man's black, weather-beaten skin. "Don't suppose you've got any ideas, do you?"

He took a deep pull on his cigarette. Coughing, he spat in the dirt and wiped the back of his hand across his moustache. "How old were you when you learned t' ride?"

I shrugged; it seemed like something I'd always known how to do. "Five. Maybe six, I guess."

"Try three and a half." He rested his thick middle against the fence which creaked under his weight. "'Course, I wouldn't expect you to remember," he said, "but your Pa – God rest his soul – he used to bring you 'round here when you weren't, oh, no taller'n my belt buckle. He'd set you up in th' saddle while me and the boys took turns walkin' the horse round the corral." He chuckled. "Damnation, but you were a sight, about as proud as a kitten with its first mouse."

I thought for a moment. "Now that you mention it," I said slowly, "I think I remember seeing a picture of me on a horse like that – a big appaloosa wasn't it?"

He nodded. "And Frank, well, he carried it in his wallet for years. Never missed an opportunity to pass it around and brag on you neither."

"So what's your point, Mister P.?"

He crushed the smoke between a calloused thumb and forefinger. "I don't expect there's a *point*, son," he said. "Jus' an old man talking, that's all." Hitching up his jeans, he walked back to the office and closed the door.

Sighing, I draped my arms across the fence. Now I really *could* see that picture, clear as if I held it in my hand. The oversized Stetson, a red checkered bandanna at my neck and the handsome calfskin vest I'd gotten for my birthday. And Dad was there too, holding the reins with a huge grin on his face. I closed my eyes, trying to remember what it felt like when I suddenly felt rough, calloused hands lift me high into a saddle. I smelled chewing tobacco, horses and ripening hay and looked down on the battered hats of Dad and his buddies. Then I spread my arms, threw back my head and laughed, a little boy on a big horse, fearless and free, like I could do anything, be anything.

Like I was . . . *ten feet tall.*

"Whoa," I said quietly, leaning against the fence to steady myself as the world swam back into focus.

Just then J.T. walked up to the fence leading Ginger by the reins. "I've about had it, Harrison," he said. "I'm doing everything you showed me but she just won't cooperate. It's hopeless."

Maybe not. "Do you remember the first time you sat on Ginger's back?" I asked him.

"Duh. I mean, it was only yesterday."

"What did it feel like?"

He frowned. "Not sure I'm following you here."

"Don't think about it, just tell me. At that moment, what did you feel? Come on, J.T., it's important."

His face told me he knew what I meant. Grinning sheepishly he said, "Okay, now it's gonna sound really dumb, but when I was sitting up there, you know, on her back, it didn't feel like Ginger and *me*. It sort of felt like . . . *us*. Like we were somehow connected with each other. Like she was a part of me and . . . and I was a part of her."

"Perfect," I said. "And that's exactly the way you've got to ride her."

"Way? What way?" He threw up his hands. "Harrison, what the hell are you talking about?"

"Okay, listen up," I said. "Ginger's not like a car or a motorcycle you can just point wherever you want to go and hit the gas. She's alive. She has a mind of her own. When you want to go left, don't just think 'I need to make her turn left,' think *we* need to go left. If you want to stop, think *we* need to stop. Voice commands and the reins will help but if you think like she's your legs she'll act like you're her brain."

J.T. thought about that for a moment. "Kind of like becoming one with the horse, huh?" he said with a weak grin. "Pretty Zen. I didn't know you guys went in for that stuff around here."

"Call it whatever you like but it works. Haven't you ever heard of horse whisperers?"

He nodded. "I think so."

"Well that's what they do; try to understand what the horse is feeling, to get into their head. If you can manage that everything else will fall into place. I promise."

He still wasn't buying it. "But it can't be that simple."

"Don't kid yourself; it isn't simple at all. It means getting inside her skin and letting her inside yours. For most people that's hard. For some it's impossible. But I think maybe, just maybe you can do it."

Not that I believed in miracles, but what I saw in those next few hours came pretty darn close. It seemed like J.T. decided to let out a breath he'd been holding for a long, long time. Ginger must have sensed it too because her own hesitation dwindled to almost nothing then vanished. Arms folded, I leaned against the fence and watched them circle the arena. Even from a distance I could almost feel their heartbeats, their breathing, their *beings* merging into one. It was so amazing that it almost hurt to watch.

I guess I felt pretty good about finding a way to reach J.T. too If I'd stuck to my original idea plan he probably wouldn't have learned much of anything. Only by trying something different had I gotten results. *That* was a new experience for me.

At dusk I dropped J.T. at the hotel and headed home. Though we had a ways to go, his confidence seemed to grow every time he climbed into the saddle. But important as that was, arena-riding was only a start. I had to know if those skills would be there when he really needed them, and there was only one way to find that out.

Early next morning Sam and I rummaged through the garage to pull together the gear I needed. It took a while but I finally found Dad's sleeping bag in an old packing crate. It hadn't been aired out since our last hunting trip and the faded cotton smelled a little musty, with a hint of the Old Spice Dad always wore.

"Hey, Cody, check this out." Sam held up a ragged-looking sack of cloth. "I found it in a box here under the workbench."

I stared at the rumpled brown fabric. Cotton leaked from the seams and a leather-button eye was missing but I recognized it right away: Tonka, the fat stuffed buffalo I played with as a kid.

"Don't think I remember seeing this before," she said, giving it a quick once-over. "What do you suppose it is?"

Years had passed since I banished Tonka from my room. After Dad's funeral I carried him out to the garage, stuffed him in an old shoe box and then pushed it under the workbench as far as my twelve-year old arms would reach. And there he had stayed till now.

Sam raised it to her nose. "Yuck, smells pretty nasty. Think we ought to trash it?"

Part of me wanted to but a bigger part wasn't so sure. "Nah," I said, "it might be one of Mom's old toys. We better not mess with it till she gets back."

She slid Tonka back where she found him. There were too many memories wrapped up in that little stuffed toy for me to handle right then. Would there ever be a time when I could?

Sam brushed dust from her hands. "Okay, sack lunches are on the front seat and I put the rest of the food in the back of the truck. The hamburgers are frozen so they ought to keep till you cook 'em. You also got foil wrapped potatoes, some eggs, coffee, jerky. Everything."

"Thanks, Sam. I really appreciate it."

She leaned against the workbench, twirling a long braid between her fingers. "Cody, do you really think this is such a good idea? So soon, that is. What if he can't handle it?"

I dragged our old cook kit into the open and blew dust from the cast-iron skillet. "I don't have much choice," I said. "But by this time tomorrow I'll know for sure."

After I dropped Sam off to stay with the Mondragon's I headed for the hotel with Zack's trailer hitched to the bumper. J.T. spotted me from his window. He leaned out dripping wet and shirtless.

"Hey, it isn't seven yet, Harrison!" he shouted, toweling his hair. "What gives?"

"Tomorrow is graduation day from the world-famous Harrison School of Horsemanship," I shouted back. "*If* you pass the final exam, that is."

"Uh-huh. What's in the trailer?"

"Zack. My horse."

"And what's with all that crap in the back of the truck?"

"That crap *is* the final exam." I pointed at my watch. "And it starts in about ten minutes so you'd better get down here pronto."

A few seconds later he burst through the front door, boots in hand and shirttail flapping. "I sure hope you grade on the curve." he said.

While J.T. mucked the few remaining stalls I saddled our horses and distributed the gear between them. About ten-thirty we mounted up, then forded the creek and rode toward the forest that loomed beyond the sage-covered hills. It was a crazy-beautiful day with a light breeze driving puffy clouds across a deep blue sky. Sunlight played across the pine-scented trail as we rode beneath the canopy of trees.

J.T. urged Ginger alongside Zack and me. "So, you gonna let me in on where we're going?" he asked.

"Don't worry," I replied. "You're going to like it."

On maps this trail was just a dotted line labeled 'Upper Kendall Loop' but it had always been a big part of my life. Every summer Dad and I hiked along the creek with our fishing rods, looking for the deeper pools where the fat rainbows lurked. In December, we snowshoed across frozen meadows, searching for the perfect Christmas tree. But fall was always my favorite. I loved the bright hazy days and crisp, starlit nights. Together we rode and camped and hunted as the aspen turned the hills to gold. In five years I hadn't set foot on this trail but I was surprised how good it felt to be riding familiar ground.

And God, I almost forgot how much I missed him.

The trail grew steeper and after a while I had J.T. ride point. A bit self-conscious at first, he soon settled confidently into the saddle, reins draped casually across his thigh. On steeper sections of the trail he still used the saddle horn to keep his balance, and once when Ginger stumbled he barely recovered. On the whole, though, he didn't ride too badly at all. I only hoped Liebowitz would see it that way too.

Around noontime we stopped at an old lightning bald on the shoulder of Kendall Peak. We turned the horses out to graze and opened our sack lunches, enjoying the cool breeze that whispered over the open meadow.

As usual, fat clouds were piling up in the west, promising afternoon storms. For a brief moment those clouds seemed to be full of ghostly shapes, like great shaggy buffalo leaping upwards into the sky. Then just like that they were gone. I rubbed my eyes and took another bite of sandwich, wondering what had I done to deserve these strange visions. That, and those nightly rides as Billy MacAllister.

J.T. wolfed his sandwich then belched loudly and stretched out on the ground. "Say, Harrison, Ben told me you lived on a ranch," he said. "The Teebar Hess, or something?"

"T Bar S." I pointed to the valley spread out below us. "See those cattle out in the meadow there? That's part of our place. The rest of it lays in a valley back up behind the trees."

He whistled. "Wow. My folks own a half acre near Fresno and I thought that was big."

"Out in your neck of the woods it probably is. But not here. Our ranch is just about the smallest one in the valley."

He bit noisily into an apple. "I've never actually been on a ranch before, a real one that is. Just some film sets in Arizona. I suppose it's gotta be a lot work."

"You could say that," I replied, remembering the broken downspout I still hadn't fixed. "Seems like it never stops sometimes."

He pointed a finger in my direction. "Okay, then how come you've got the time to teach a little prick like me to ride?"

"Oh, you're not all *that* little," I said, dodging the apple core he threw at my head. "Besides, Ben's finally got me on the payroll so I'm not just doing this for fun. And as far as tending cattle . . ." I shrugged. "Right now we don't have any."

He looked puzzled. "But you said —"

"Those animals I showed you don't belong to us. See, we lease our pastures to the Dee Double Vee. The cattle are theirs. I mean, it wasn't anything we wanted to do but I guess it all started after my Dad died."

J.T. shook his head. "Sorry to hear that, man."

I sensed he wanted to know what happened. Everyone did but in a strange way I felt more at ease talking to J.T. than to my friends who asked the same thing. Besides, after a few days we'd probably never see each other again so what did it matter? Taking a deep breath, I continued.

"When I was twelve my Dad and I were out hunting elk, like we'd done every fall for years. But when we were late returning a search party came after us. They found our camp but, well, my Dad was dead. Gunshot wound in the chest. I was okay but I couldn't tell them what happened."

"Wait a minute." J.T. raised himself on one elbow. "You were there but you didn't see it?"

"I must have but I couldn't remember. It felt like I was in, I don't know, a kind of fog or something. Mom was pretty freaked so she took me to this therapist lady over in Durango. She told me that sometimes when you see something that's too horrible your brain kind of blocks it out so you don't have to re-live it over and over. And as far as Sheriff Ruiz, he checked both of us for gunpowder residue and found nothing. All he knew for sure was that the bullet came from Dad's gun. So he just called it an accident and closed the case."

J.T. shook his head. "Then I guess you'll never know, huh?"

"Not exactly," I replied. "According to this therapist, everything I saw is still there in my head, just sort of locked away. All I have to do is find the key."

As the day passed it was hard not to think about what I told J.T. at lunch. Was there really some kind of magic key waiting to unlock my past? Although I'd thought about it a lot right after Dad died, in truth I'd pretty much given up looking. So why was I thinking about it now? I pulled out my bandanna and mopped my forehead. Who knew? Maybe it came from seeing old Tonka again. Maybe it was those ghostly shapes in the clouds or Billy's nightly ride through my dreams. Whatever the reason, I wondered if I'd even recognize this key when I saw it.

Lightning flickered on the horizon. "Let's get a move on," I said. "We've still got a few miles to cover and I don't want to get caught in the open."

The mountains hereabouts were full of rotting,

tumbledown buildings left over from the gold mining days. I hoped to camp in an old prospector's shack I knew but with lightning darting overhead that chance was fast slipping away. A wind blew up out of nowhere, cold and smelling like rain. Fat raindrops peppered the trail and soaked our shoulders. Then a lightning bolt sizzled through the trees. I winced and counted: *one-one thousand, two-one thousand, three* . . .

Thunder boomed as if it was coming from somewhere deep underground. And close. God, *way* too close. "Come on!" I shouted. "We gotta make a run for it!"

We urged our horses to a trot, then a gallop. I was relieved to hear J.T. and Ginger pounding along right behind me. For a while we even seemed to be getting ahead of the storm.

"Stay close as you can," I yelled over the wind, "and keep a tight rein in case —"

A blinding flash ripped the world apart. I threw a hand before my eyes and saw the dark shadows of bones. A crack of thunder pounded my eardrums and splinters filled the air, thick as angry hornets. Terrified, Zack reared up and I slipped from the saddle. As I hit the ground something dug into my side; I gasped at the hot stab of pain. Blood, warm and coppery, filled my mouth. I felt I was about to pass out when Zack's reins brushed my cheek. Without thinking I grabbed the rain-slick leather and struggled to my feet just as another stroke of lightning blasted down a hundred feet away. Startled, Zack jerked suddenly and pulled me off my feet. I slammed against a tree; stars danced at the edge of my vision as I hung on the edge of blackness again.

"Zack!" I jerked his bridle. "You stop it! Stop it *NOW!*"

A curtain of rain closed around us. Although Zack snorted and pawed the ground I sensed the fear draining out of him. "Easy there, easy," I whispered, stroking his neck. "You're okay."

Each word turned a knife between my ribs. Blood welled from the corner of my mouth and dripped slowly off my chin. But it wasn't me I worried about; J.T. and Ginger were nowhere to be seen. Panic rose in my gut but I fought it down. They could only have gone the way we came, so I mounted up and started back, calling out in the faint hope they'd hear me.

Rushing water covered the ground, splashing around broken tree limbs. Every few feet, small muddy landslides forced us off the trail and into the dripping trees. Long minutes passed. I felt suddenly dizzy and short of breath. Sourness crowded my throat.

"Whoa." I croaked then half-fell from the saddle and dropped to my knees. Retching, I spilled my stomach onto the trail, choking and puking till there was nothing left to bring up. Cold air pressed against my face. For a brief, terrible moment I saw myself on the edge of a ravine, looking down at J.T. and Ginger, their twisted bodies lit by flashes of lightning. Breathing into my cupped hands I forced the thought from my head, mounted up and rode on.

A large aspen, freshly uprooted, lay completely across the trail. As Zack picked his way around the tree I thought I saw a shadowy form heading toward us.

"Sweet Jesus," I whispered, "let it be them." Seconds later we stood side by side with J.T. and Ginger. J.T.'s hair matted his face like thin brown cobwebs. He was bloody too, from a cut on his forehead. Ginger was mud-caked from ears to hooves but I'd seldom seen anything so good in my whole life.

"Are you okay?" I said through chattering teeth.

"*We're* okay," J.T. said as he stroked Ginger's neck. "And I've had just about enough g-goddam excitement for one day, Harrison."

By the time we reached the miner's shack the storm had blown itself out. For just a moment the sun reappeared, bathing the forest in light as it sank toward the horizon. Raindrops dripped from the trees, sparkling like tiny diamonds. Fortunately it hadn't rained much here. We rolled stones into a ring then scrounged up some dry wood and kindled a roaring fire.

I lashed a rope above the flames so J.T. and I could dry our rain-soaked clothes. When I unbuttoned my shirt

I found my ribcage red and swollen, streaked with tracks of dried and matted blood.

J.T. winced when he saw the damage. "Ouch," he said, unlacing his boots. "How'd you get that?"

"Zack bucked me off and I hit a rock," I said painfully as I slipped out of my shirt. "Doesn't feel like anything's broken, but I'm betting it's going to hurt for a while."

"A long while by the looks of it." J.T. stepped out of his jeans and dropped them in a soggy pile at his feet. "And did you say you fell off?"

"*Bucked* off," I replied. "There's a big difference, you know."

"So you say." J.T. draped his jeans across the rope. "I managed to stay in the saddle the whole time." He pulled off his boxers and wrung them out. "Soon as I'm warmed up I'll tell you all about it."

We stood naked before the flames, too cold for even the sneaky locker-room glances guys use to check each other out. The crackling heat felt great against my goosepimply skin. As the logs burned to glowing coals we wrapped ourselves in scratchy woolen blankets and hunkered around the fire to start dinner. Soon potatoes hissed beneath the embers. J.T. offered to cook the rest of the meal, so as hamburgers sizzled he told me about his little afternoon adventure. Without exaggerating, of course.

"When that lightning hit, Ginger jumped five feet straight up," he said, holding the pan over the flames. "And when she landed, oh, man, that's when the shit really hit the fan." He balanced the skillet between two rocks then stood and drew the blanket around his body. Shadows danced from the soles of his feet as he paced around the fire. "And once Ginger hit the ground I knew I couldn't stop her. Hell, we tore off so fast I never had a chance to see what happened to you two."

"Right. And you're telling me you didn't fall off?"

He grinned. "Nope. Came real close but I remembered what you told me about getting inside Ginger's skin. Feeling what she's feeling. When I felt how scared she was I realized I was pretty scared too. Since she was doing all the work I just held on for the ride." Kneeling, he slid a burger onto a paper plate, added a baked potato and handed it over. "Remember where that tree was lying across the trail?"

I nodded and took a bite of meat. Streams of warm, wonderful juice dribbled down my chin.

J.T. held his arms wide. "Ginger cleared that sucker in one leap," he said. "One! It felt like we were flying. I mean, it was better than the first time I had sex."

That was just a little too much. "Let's see," I said. "Would that have been with your left hand or your right?"

"Okay, left," he said with a grin. "But it was that

good, Harrison. I swear."

I laughed, ignoring the sharp twinge in my side. He held out his cup and I poured him some coffee. "Even ol' Ben would have been proud of me, don't you think?"

That reminded me of something I'd wondered about since J.T. got here. "Speaking of Ben." I said, "How come you lied to him about being able to ride? What was that all about?"

J.T. shoveled in a forkful of potato. "Well, after the audition he asked if I knew how. I didn't, but I figured hey, how hard could it be? So I told him I could."

I laid another log on the fire and watched flames curl around it, hungrily seeking dry patches on the wood. "Didn't you think anyone would notice? If you're playing a cowboy it wouldn't be an easy thing to fake."

He licked burger grease off his fingers. "Let me explain a few things," he said. "See, when I was eight I had a sitcom on Nickelodeon: *And Davey Makes Three.* It had a decent run but by the time it got cancelled I'd pretty much outgrown my cute stage. Except for a few commercials nothing else came along. Everyone said I was hard to work with and, well, maybe they were right. Then last month I get busted with a joint some guy gave me at a party in Malibu. It was my second possession so I figured on a thirty-day sleep-over at L.A. County Youth. But my lawyer cut a deal: stay clean till I'm eighteen and I'm home free."

"My Dad would have locked me in the cellar and fed me through the keyhole."

"Mine probably should have," said J.T. "But instead I get stuck in a support group with a bunch of other losers. We just sat around whining about our problems."

"I hear you," I said. The few support groups Mom made me attend hadn't done much for me either.

J.T. looked up. "You know those creepy tabloids, the ones in the check-out lines? Guys like me usually end up on the front cover: 'Former Child Star Dies of Overdose' or some shit like that. I figured I was gonna be next but then my agent heard about this Billy MacAllister part. I read against a dozen other actors and about freaked when Ben offered it to me. It's not a big picture but it's a terrific part. He got me cheap too. But I knew it would really help my career if I pulled it off."

"Provided you knew how to ride."

"Right. But when you get offered a role this good, you say 'Ride? Why of *course* I can ride, Mr. Liebowitz.' Then you bust your hump learning how before shooting starts. I just put off the learning part way too long."

"So the short of it is, you lied to get a job."

J.T. frowned, then rolled out his sleeping bag and crawled inside. "It's not just a *job*," he said. "Christ, it's a way for me to get my life back. I've always loved to act but I thought my career was over. Ben's taking a big chance on me and I'll be damned if I'm going to screw it up. It might be my last. I mean, haven't you ever wanted something so bad you'd do anything to make it happen?"

"Once," I said slowly, spreading my bag out on the other side of the fire. "But it was a pretty long time ago."

"Details, details. Come on, Harrison, I told you mine."

Kneeling, I tossed another log on the fire. What could it hurt? "Well, raising cattle has always been a tough business," I said, "and the prices we got were lousy and always getting worse. So one day Dad just up and packs his bedroll and rides off into the mountains. See, he always did stuff like that when he had a problem he couldn't solve or a big decision to make. Then two days later he rides back all excited and says we're going to try something different: raising buffalo."

"I've had buffalo *fajitas*," he offered. "Cost more but they were sure worth it."

Just talking about buffalo again was kind of exciting. "Anyway, Dad and I visited this buffalo ranch in Nebraska. He planned to take on some calves the next spring but, well, we had a lot of financial problems after he died. We lost our herd and barely kept hold of the ranch. There just wasn't money left for anything else."

"I get that part. But why did *you* give it up?"

Wasn't he listening? "We couldn't – that is, I just didn't have a choice, that's all. Sometimes life screws you over and there's nothing you can do about it."

He yawned. "I guess. But if you really wanted to raise buffalo as bad as you say —"

I stood. "Just drop it," I told him. "It was a stupid idea then and it's a stupid idea now. It never would have worked out. So let's not talk about it anymore, okay?"

"Okay, okay." J.T. hunkered down into his sleeping bag. "But I gotta tell you, it didn't sound so stupid to me."

After a last check on the horses I banked the fire and set a pot of water by the coals for tomorrow's coffee. I felt myself shivering but I knew it wasn't just the night-time chill; J.T.'s unanswered question still hung in the air. Why *had* I given it up?

Exhausted, I slid into my sleeping bag and cupped hands behind my head. Above me the rising moon flirted with silvery clouds. Once Dad was gone all of my buffalo-dreams vanished like campfire sparks in the night; were they really still possible? I rubbed my eyes. I'd better be careful; it was dangerous to start thinking like Sam.

"By the way," I said with a yawn. "You passed the final exam."

No one answered. J.T. Kelley was sound asleep.

"Get your lazy butt up, Harrison."

I opened my eyes and saw J.T. learning over me. He handed me a steaming mug of coffee. "I found some eggs in Ginger's pack," he said and nodded towards the fire. "You can have 'em any way you want so long as it's scrambled."

I drained the coffee, enjoying its dark warmth. Overhead the sky stretched a deep cloudless blue. My ribs still ached from yesterday, but the pain was dull and manageable. Yawning, I pulled on my smoke-scented jeans and traipsed into the bushes to pee.

After breakfast we packed up our gear for the ride home. J.T. took point as we headed down through the rain-washed forest. Soon the warm sunshine and Zack's rolling gait ganged up on my eyelids.

J.T. glanced over his shoulder. "Hey, you doing okay back there?" he asked. "You don't look so good."

"I'm okay. I just didn't get too much sleep last night, that's all. My bag was really soaked."

"Well, let me know if you want to stop for a while."

The night had been miserable all right but it wasn't the soggy bag or my throbbing ribcage or even the tree root that poked me in the back every time I twitched. It was my dreams again, only this time Billy was nowhere to be found; it was just me and Zack alone on the trail, driving a single enormous buffalo before us.

It was Tonka.

God, he was huge, big as a school bus and he swaggered down the trail like he owned it. But despite his size he was still my stuffed animal. Wads of cotton leaked from seams in his corduroy hide and a leather-button eye the size of a hubcap lolled back and forth on one side of his head.

The scenery had changed too. Instead of rolling sagebrush we were surrounded by white-barked aspen, somewhere high in the mountains. The trees opened into a meadow with a couple of abandoned buildings in the distance. Alone now, I rode down what must have been the main street, overgrown with aspen saplings and scraggly weeds. False-fronts looked down on me and I sensed something – or someone – in the shadows. Hidden, but not exactly hiding. More like . . . *waiting*. There was something vaguely familiar about those buildings too.

"Dammit, Harrison, is this where we cross or not?"

My eyes snapped open. I must have nodded off again because we were already at the west bank of Tohachi Creek.

"Uh, here's fine," I said and followed him and Ginger through the swirling water.

In the distance I saw a red convertible parked in the Ayo-Kay lot. A figure leaned against the hood, half-hidden behind a newspaper. I urged Zack alongside Ginger and J.T.

"Want to race?" I pointed toward the figure, who by this time had caught sight of us. "C'mon, what say we show old Ben he got his money's worth."

J.T. grinned, then turned his cap backwards and gathered up the reins. "Okay, on three," he said. "One . . . two . . ."

"Three!" I shouted, and we were off.

J.T. crouched low and kept his head close to Ginger's neck as he urged her on. We ran together for a hundred yards but I backed off ever so slightly before we reached the Ayo-Kay gate. J.T. forged ahead then shot one arm straight up in the air. He peeled a tight three-sixty around Liebowitz' car while the bald-headed man stared, open-mouthed.

I followed the two of them back to town then we waited outside the hotel while J.T. packed up his stuff. For once, the producer seemed in a pretty good mood.

"It's better than I could have hoped for," he said, lighting up a fresh cigar. "That first night you sure painted a grim picture. I was plenty worried, I can tell you that."

"It wasn't pretty," I agreed. "And that was even before he decided to land on my back."

"So how did you manage to turn it around? So fast, I mean." Liebowitz grinned. "You some kind of miracle worker?"

"Not hardly. Truth is, once J.T. lightened up and stopped worrying, everything sort of took care of itself. Now he's still kinda green, but that'll pass."

"Don't worry. He's had some tough times but he's really a damn fine actor. He'll make a great Billy MacAllister."

"Speaking of Billy," I said, leaning against the Caddy. "How come you're making a film about him?"

"Mainly because I can afford it." He grinned. "The book rights were cheap and with any luck I'm gonna bring it in under two million."

"That the only reason?"

Liebowitz stroked his chin. "Well, I was born in Munich," he said, "just before the end of the war. Do you know how many German Jews lived through it? Less than one in five. My parents were among the lucky ones but they knew the future lay in America. It took years to process our immigration papers so in the meantime my father read to us at night to teach us English. Westerns, mostly. God, how that man loved Westerns: Buffalo Bill, Zane Grey, *The Virginian* . . . "

"Nothing like the classics," I said.

He chuckled. "And one about a young cowboy named Billy MacAllister; it was my favorite, you see. Those first years after the war were pretty bad; bombed out buildings, no electricity or heat and hardly any food. But every night when I went to bed I thought about Billy – everything he faced – and to this day I think he gave me the strength to keep going. Eventually we made it to Los Angeles. My father found work at Paramount and well, here I am."

He was silent for a couple of moments then said "Anyway, I swore one day I'd find a way to repay Billy. I guess this is it."

I thought about telling Liebowitz about my own goings-on with Billy but decided against it; I wasn't sure how much of that I wanted to spread around. Just then the hotel door burst open and J.T. appeared with his aluminum suitcases.

"Hey, Harrison," he said, "you want to give me a hand with these again?"

While we loaded up the Caddy's trunk, J.T. headed to the Circle K to pick up road snacks. Liebowitz slid his plump body into the driver's seat then reached out and shook my hand. "Like I said before, kid, I really owe you for this one."

"Uh, speaking of owing," I said, rubbing my fingers together.

"What, you think I forgot? Ben Liebowitz never forgets." He made a show of thumbing through the pile of loose papers on the front seat. "But, ah, I was wondering if you might be interested in another arrangement."

I didn't like the sound of that. "Such as . . . ?"

"How'd you like a point? One per cent of the profits. Net, of course. J.T.'s in for points along with the other talent. Could be worth a lot in the long run with foreign sales, Netflix, DVDs and so on. For every million we clear you could end up with ten K in your pocket."

Ten thousand dollars? "You're kidding, right?"

"Could be more, could be nothing." Liebowitz took another slow pull on his cigar. "You never know, kid. In this business you never know."

Although I was tempted, there was something a little fishy about it. Okay, maybe he was grateful, but why be this generous? "Really appreciate it, Ben," I said, "but I think I'll pass. I know I'll probably kick myself tomorrow but I guess I'm not real good at taking chances."

He sifted through the papers again. "Suit yourself, kid. One chance to a customer."

After a minute it hit me. "There isn't a check for me, is there, Ben?"

Liebowitz rubbed his forehead. "No, but let me explain –"

"What's to explain? We had a deal! I-I worked my ass off teaching J.T. to ride and nearly got killed doing it! I helped you when you needed it and now you're going to cheat –"

Liebowitz got out of the car and slammed the door. "Now you look here, kid. Forty years in this business and I've never, *EVER*, cheated anyone out of a cent. It's just that I've got a little cash flow problem at the moment. Take me up on the point or I'll try to get you paid off in a couple of weeks. Or you can quit like we originally agreed."

Quickly he scribbled some numbers on a scrap of paper. "Here's our motel in Las Cruces; we're starting the shoot down there in the next few days. Ryder Production Services will be here in a day or so to start work on the set. If I don't hear from you I'll figure we got a deal."

Fuming, I drove home hotter than a bowl of red chili. It was one thing for Sam to be suckered but I should have known better. Now what choice did I have; keep working and trust Liebowitz to make good or cut my losses and quit. That was a no-brainer: I was *out*.

Exhausted, I hit the sack right after dinner, but in the middle of the night I woke to the crunch of gravel in our driveway. Shivering, I stumbled to the window and saw a large panel truck followed by a pickup pulling some kind of trailer. Three shadowy figures stood around the hood of the larger truck studying a map with flashlights.

It wasn't unusual for tourists to stop for directions, but not in the middle of the night. "You folks lost?" I called down.

The tallest figure turned and caught me in the beam of his flashlight. I shielded my eyes till the light clicked off. "Sorry about that," said a deep voice. "But is this the Harrison place?"

Still half asleep, I wasn't about to volunteer information to a shadow in my driveway. "Depends on who's asking," I said.

The shadow turned the flashlight on himself. "I'm Bob Gallegos. We're Ben Liebowitz' contractors."

"You're Ryder Production Services?"

The guy nodded. "That's us: me and my brothers. Ben said you'd help us find the site so grab your clothes and let's go, amigo."

I was tempted to tell them to go screw themselves but it probably wouldn't be fair to drag them into my hassle with Liebowitz. At least I could get them to the set. "Okay," I said. "Hang on and I'll be right down."

After I pulled on some clothes I scribbled a note for Sam. Sound sleeper that she was, she'd be fine till I got back. By the time I locked the front door and stepped outside, the shadows had piled back in the cab. A funky odor of smoke and stale coffee drifted from the open door; it smelled like a den of bears with nicotine habits.

"Uh, maybe I'd better ride in the pickup," I said, glancing around.

"No need," said Bob, who was driving. "Plenty of room in here, amigo." He turned to the shadow next to him. "We can fit this skinny little gringo in here, right Luis?"

"He don't look all that skinny to me. What do you think, Jimmy?"

Silently, the last shadow reached out a huge hand and hauled me into the cab. As the truck jerked into motion I tried to make a place for myself, but between the four of us and the gearshift there wasn't much room. Even for a skinny little gringo like me.

Soon Luis and Jimmy were snoring. At every pothole a spring poked through the worn seat cover and jabbed me in the butt. That was about the only thing keeping me awake. My eyelids drooped till I spotted a deer frozen in our headlights.

"Look out!" I yelled.

"*Madre Dios!*" Bob cranked the wheel. Branches raked the side of the cab and we missed the buck by inches. Jimmy and Luis didn't stir. "Good eyes, amigo," Bob said, steering us back onto the road. "*Muchas gracias.*"

"*De nada,*" I mumbled.

Dawn soon crept over the distant mountains. Fog drifted down the forested hills in a silvery blanket, hiding all but the tops of the tallest trees. Grunting, Jimmy and Luis roused themselves and lit cigarettes. Smoke filled the cab but I was too polite to start coughing my head off. When we finally reached the end of the road I saw mounds of black tarpaulins covering the supplies I'd arranged: piles of lumber; bags of cement; hardware of every shape and description, all charged to Liebowitz Productions of Hollywood, California.

As they got out I took stock of them through the windshield. By day they looked a lot less intimidating. Bob stood six feet or better, narrow-hipped and broad shouldered but with a smiling, pleasant face. Luis was a bit shorter but looked like his brother, right down to the faded flannel shirt and iron-gray ponytail. Jimmy was apparently the runt of the litter. Short, with a huge belly, he had a comical, almost penguin-like waddle.

They strolled away from the truck, pointing here and there as they argued and laughed and shouted in Spanish. Stretching, I stepped down from the cab and filled my lungs, grateful for a taste of fresh air.

"Leave it to *mis tíos* to forget I'm alive," said a voice behind me.

Surprised, I spun and saw a tall, dark-eyed girl — obviously someone had to be driving the pickup. She wore a white tank top over a pair of faded blue jeans with the knees worn out. On her feet were scuffed black motorcycle boots and a wallet chain followed the curve of her thigh. As the wind caught her long black hair she smiled at me. And God, was she ever good at it.

She held out her hand. "Angel Suarez."

Her voice was husky, almost boyish and it curled around me like smoke from burning leaves. A slight chip in her front tooth gave her words a little whistle, mysterious and sexy as all get out. As we shook hands, my knees felt just a little goofy. "Hi. I'm, uh, that is, my name is Cody . . ."

"Harrison. I know." Angel hooked thumbs in her belt. "Awesome," she said, breathing deeply. "I've never been to a place where you can do this without gagging."

She ran her fingers through her hair which fell across her bare shoulders in inky shimmering waves. Angel's brown eyes were wide-set below thick eyebrows and her cheekbones were just a bit too high to be called beautiful. I noticed she wasn't all soft and curvy either. But to my way of thinking the pieces came together just exactly right.

Our eyes met. "So I hear you and I are going to be working together," she said. "Right?"

"Uh . . . sure," I heard myself say. "I-I reckon we are." A whistle split the air. Bob and Luis motioned us to join them. As we walked toward the tarpaulins Angel elbowed me in the arm.

"Okay, cowboy," she said. "Here's a little free advice. Bob runs the show but don't take your eyes off Jimmy for a minute. If you're going to have trouble that's where it'll come from." She squeezed the back of my neck. "Got it?"

"Sure," I mumbled. "Thanks."

Bob sat atop a pile of lumber, rubbing his hands. "All right," he said. "Since you *niños* have gotten acquainted let's get a move on. We've got us a town to build."

As the day passed I got a quick and dirty introduction to set-building, Gallegos-brothers style. While Bob and Luis huddled over some plans, Jimmy led me to the piles of supplies. I looked around for Angel but she seemed to have disappeared.

"Okay, the first thing you gotta do," Jimmy said as he gestured with his clipboard, "is to get all this stuff organized."

To me, it looked like it already was. "What's the matter with the way it is now?"

He glared at me. "You got a problem following instructions?" He propped the clipboard against his pudgy thigh. "Tell me now if you do."

"Uh, no. But —"

"Good, 'cause I damn sure hate repeating myself."

I followed him through the maze of supplies while he barked orders like a drill sergeant. "Divide this load here into piles: two-bys and four-bys, no more than ten boards high. See those furring strips there? Get 'em up off the ground and onto a couple of blocks so they don't warp. Then stack the plywood with the finished side down."

Remembering Angel's advice I just smiled and said "No problem, Mr. Gallegos."

He scowled and parked his pencil behind one ear. "*Mister* Gallegos is *mi padre*," he said. "The hired help calls me Jimmy, understand?"

"Sure," I said, "Uh, Jimmy."

The scowl softened into a frown. "That's better. Now where's that girl? Angel! ANGEL!"

In a few minutes we found the missing Angel in the back of the panel truck, curled up on a pile of padded blankets. She opened one eye. "Come on, Uncle Jimmy," she groaned, covering her face, "give me a break. I haven't slept in almost two days."

"A break? You're the one who wanted to come along, *chiquita mia*. If you wanted to sleep you should have listened to me and stayed home. I told you this is no place for a girl."

She gave us a cavernous yawn. "Oh please, let's not start on that again. I'm already here."

"Only 'cause I was outvoted." Jimmy nodded

towards Bob and Luis. "But that don't mean you get a *siesta* whenever you feel like it. We got work to do, starting now. Pull your weight or you ain't nothing but excess baggage."

To emphasize his point he whacked her in the rear end with his clipboard. I winced; it probably didn't hurt but it bothered me just the same.

"Okay, okay. I'm up." She stepped down from the truck and stretched. Her arms were long and lean, tanned to perfection.

"And see that you stay that way," Jimmy said. "Help the boy here set the lumber up. He knows what I want. Then when you're done I need this hardware sorted. Every last nut and bolt. Use the buckets in the truck to keep it all straight. If I need a ten-penny nail I don't want to have to search through a dozen goddamn boxes to find it. We good?"

Angel and I looked at each other and nodded. "*Bueno.* Now get yourselves busy."

As we sorted the supplies I tried to convince myself I'd changed my mind just to give Liebowitz another chance. That I believed in him and trusted him not to cheat me. That this movie thing was going to be a rip-roaring success and make us all rich. But even I didn't believe those arguments; it was the chance to work with Angel, plain and simple.

Right off I noticed little things about her. Beads of

perspiration that glistened like diamonds on her cheek. A turquoise stud that sat in a perfectly formed ear. Even the thin white scar tracing the bottom of her chin; I wondered how she got it. Each was kind of fascinating in its own way, like pieces of a puzzle too complicated to admire all at once.

And man, could that girl work. She swung lumber like a pro, handling loads as big as I could manage. Next to her I had all the grace God gave a cow as my Dad used to say.

As the day grew hotter, perspiration soaked through Angel's top and formed dark patches where the fabric clung to her skin. Now and then her shirt rode up and revealed a glimpse of tanned, flat stomach. I tried not to stare but it was a losing battle.

Around noon we broke for lunch. While her uncles stretched out under the trees, Angel and I headed into town to score some food. On the way Angel massaged the back of her neck, working a hand up and under that long black hair. God, how I wanted to say: 'here, let me do that'. I pictured my hands on her shoulders, soothing her tense muscles. She'd moan softly and say . . .

"Damn, I think I could sleep for a week."

My eyes snapped open. "Uh, what?"

She yawned. "After a thousand miles I've about had it. We weren't supposed to get here till tomorrow but Bob decided to drive straight through. Last night I drank so much coffee I thought I would pee espresso."

"You know, I could drive," I said as I pictured her lying on the seat, head snuggled comfortably in my lap. "If you'd like, that is."

"Thanks, but I'll manage. I think I just need me some tunes."

She reached under the seat and pulled out a box full of CDs. We hit a bump and the cases scattered across the floor. "Shit," she said, bending over. "Here, hold the wheel."

As I leaned over my chest pressed lightly, briefly against her back. I felt the damp warmth of her body through my shirt. *Oh Lord take me now; let me die happy.*

One by one Angel pitched the CDs into my lap then took the wheel again. "I can never decide," she said. "Why don't you pick something."

It was quite a collection. Beyoncé, *Pet Sounds* – an old Beach Boys album – and the new Justin Bieber CD, still in the wrapper. Unsure what to choose I just grabbed the one that looked like it got the most use. Seconds later the voice of sweet, dead Selena echoed from the tinny speakers behind the seat.

Angel nodded her head in time with the music, mouthing the words to *Amor Prohibita* as her hands rapped lightly against the wheel. "Excellent," she finally allowed. It came out *exsssselent* and I felt all warm and goofy again. She favored me with a sly grin. "And here I thought all you cowboys hated *Tejano*."

All you cowboys? "What's that supposed to mean?" I asked.

She looked sideways at me. "Don't you rednecks usually go for that country and western shit?"

I frowned. "I'm no redneck."

"You're a cowboy, right? I see you got the boots and the hat."

"But you're wearing boots too."

"Okay," she admitted, "but yours are the pointy kind and that makes you a cowboy in my book. And besides, every cowboy I've ever met is a redneck deep down inside."

It pissed me off to hear that but I knew who she meant; guys my age who hung around bars they were too young to get into, dipping Skoal and raising hell with anyone whose skin was just a shade or two darker than theirs. Still, I resented the way she jumped to conclusions about me and told her so.

She shrugged. "You think you're different, huh? Didn't know there was more than one kind of cowboy."

"Seems to be a lot of things you don't know."

"Like what?"

"Like how to get to town. Hang a left here."

Angel swore and cranked the wheel hard. My seat belt tightened and gravel chattered against the wheel well till she steered back onto the road. "Hey, a little more warning would be nice," she snapped.

"Then maybe you should open your mouth and ask," I shot back. First J.T. now Angel. Jesus, did everyone from the city come with a built-in attitude problem?

After a mile or two of chilly silence Angel took a deep breath and blew it softly between her teeth. "Don't suppose you've ever been to L.A., have you?" she asked.

"Not hardly."

"Believe it or not, I've never been away from it till now. Colorado is a first for me." She chewed her lip. "Hey, no offense here, but where I live it's not a good idea to let down your guard till you find out where you stand. Not good and not healthy, either."

"Fair enough, but you mind telling me what I was doing to bother you so much?"

Angel brushed a speck of dirt off her jeans. "Well, you kept staring at me."

Blood rushed to my cheeks. I'd been so busy sneaking glances at her it never occurred to me she might be sneaking them back. "No, I-I wasn't," I said.

She waved me off. "Oh, bullshit. Come on, every time I turned around you were checking me out. Don't you dare lie. You were, right?"

"I guess maybe it looked like that," I said, fumbling for words, "but I wasn't, uh, staring."

"Oh no? Then what do you call it around here?"

"Uh, maybe I was just kind of . . . of *watching* you."

Angel shook her head. "Watching, staring. What's the difference?"

I thought for a moment; say the wrong thing here and I'd be permanently lumped in with *all you cowboys*. "I guess if I was doing it because I thought you were, you know, really hot or you had this totally fine body, now that would be staring."

She looked confused. "So you don't think I'm hot or have a —"

Shit. "No, no, no, what I meant is that I was just watching you work."

"Oh give me a break."

"No, I'm serious. I mean, the way you picked up all that lumber without losing your balance and the way you carried it around, so smooth that is, and just the way you walked and, and . . ." My voice trailed off as I ran out of reasons. It sounded so totally, incredibly lame that I grit my teeth, waiting for her to call me a liar again.

She thought for a moment. "Gotta admit that's the first time I've heard that one," she said, but her voice sounded softer, like she almost wanted to believe me but hadn't quite made up her mind. A gust of wind caught her hair. It whipped momentarily across her face as if beckoning me to touch it, hold it . . .

"Nothing else?" she asked.

I shook my head and glanced quickly out the side window. Other than a sudden desire to run barefoot and naked through that hair I couldn't think of a single thing. Angel said nothing but when I looked back a few moments later she was smiling.

We stopped at the Dairy Treet outside of town. While Angel lined up for the food I headed to the pay phone to call Sam. "And where were you at five-thirty this morning?" my sister snapped when she heard my voice.

"Calm down," I said. "I left you a note. Besides, what were you doing up that early anyway?"

"Mom called. Uncle Lou isn't doing much better so she's going to stay a few more weeks to help Aunt Carol. She said she faxed the papers to Liebowitz and wanted to know how things were going. And you owe me big time for covering your butt, Cody. Now where are you, and what's up?"

It took a couple of minutes but I filled her in on the details. Most of them, anyway.

"So what made you change your mind about taking the job?" she asked. "You sounded dead-set against it last night at dinner."

"Hey, aren't you the one always saying I should try new things?"

She laughed. "Sure, but when the heck do you ever listen to me?"

I felt an elbow in my side. "Come on, cowboy," Angel said. "We've only got an hour for lunch so let's get a move on while this stuff's still hot."

Quickly I put my hand over the phone, hoping Sam hadn't heard. "Sure. Just give me a minute, okay?" As Angel headed for the door I put the phone back to my ear.

"Who was that?" Sam asked.

"Nobody," I whispered, making sure Angel wasn't in earshot. "And –"

"Nobody, my rear end. Come on, Cody, what's her name?"

"Look, I'll be home by six, so you better –"

"Don't leave me hanging like this!" Sam cried. "What does she look like? I mean, is she really cute?"

"Hanging up now," I said, and did.

Angel sat on the passenger side of the truck and as I opened the driver's door she tossed me the keys. "Believe I'll take you up on that offer," she said with a yawn. "Guess I really could use a little nap."

As I slipped behind the wheel she toed off her boots and stretched out, joints popping. Her white-stockinged feet plopped in my lap. She wiggled her toes. "Don't worry, they're clean."

Right then I wouldn't have cared if she'd stepped in a fresh pile of horse manure. She snuggled into the seat, shifting her weight to get comfortable. Her heels pressed the inside of my thighs and the air in the cab felt suddenly warm and close.

"Oh," she added, "better not touch the fries or Jimmy'll tear you a new one."

I glanced down at her feet. French fries were about the last thing I wanted get my hands on right then but I just said "got it" and gunned the truck out of the parking lot and into the bright Colorado sun.

Angel drove me home that first night and I only avoided an interrogation by dozing off at the dinner table. But next morning as I drove Sam to a babysitting job she didn't hesitate giving me the third degree.

"'I was watching the way you work'?" she said, spreading her arms. "Oh my God, that's what you told her? Talk about lame. I mean, stuff like that makes me embarrassed to admit you're my brother."

"So what was I supposed to say?"

"Well, do you like her?" I nodded. "Then what's the big deal? Just tell her."

"But that's the problem, Sam. Every time I try to think of something to say it's like the words get screwed up by the time they reach my mouth. I end up sounding like a total dork."

Sam shook her head. "You guys kill me. It's so stupid worrying about picking the right words. Just tell her the truth. Even if the words aren't fancy she'll at least know you're being honest. Now come on, think. What's the very first thing you remember about her?"

That was easy. "Her voice," I said as we turned into the Ramierez' driveway. "Sam, I swear to God she has the most wonderful voice you've ever heard. It's totally amazing."

Sam opened the door. "I'll bet no one's ever told her that before," she said. "But if that's what you feel, then that's what you go with." She punched my shoulder. "Just don't drool on yourself, okay? I've got a reputation to think of."

I reached the set about a quarter after eight. In the meadow stood a large open-sided work tent with the faded words 'Hermosillo Mortuary' stenciled across the top. A coffee pot steamed on a battered Coleman stove and I helped myself to a cup before looking around. The tent was full of electric saws, a drill press and a few machines I'd never seen before. Fluorescent lights hung from the ceiling, linked by spaghetti-like bundles of wire.

Jimmy stepped into the tent. He glanced at his watch then back at me with narrowed eyes. "You're late," he snapped.

Here it comes. "Sorry, Jimmy. Guess I might have overslept a little bit."

"Around here we start at eight, not eight-fifteen. We clear on that?"

"Eight. Right. It won't happen again."

"See that it don't. Everyone gets one screw-up. This was yours. Make it your last."

Grumbling, he passed Angel on her way in. She poured herself some coffee. "Congratulations, cowboy. Second day on the job and you've already made Jimmy's shit list." She grinned. "But don't worry, I'll probably be joining you in a day or so."

When she blew on the coffee to cool it that faint little whistle sent shivers down my spine. Casually, I sidled up next to her. "Look," I began, "about what I said yesterday . . ."

Angel waved me off. "No, forget it," she said. "It was kind of cute. Though I gotta admit 'I was watching you work' isn't what I'm used to hearing. Usually it's 'hey *mamasita*, c'mere and let me make you a woman' or some crap like that. It was a nice change. Sort of."

Go on, tell her. I cleared my throat. "Well, there *was* something else," I said. "Uh, has anyone ever told you that you've got this really wonderful –"

"There you are!" Bob bustled into the tent with Jimmy right on his heels. "See?" he said to his brother. "I knew our little amigo wouldn't let us down."

"He was late," Jimmy growled.

"He's young. He'll learn." Bob laid a hand on my

shoulder. "And I'm sure he plans to work extra hard to make up for it, right?"

His grip left little room for argument. As he hustled me out of the tent I glanced over my shoulder and saw Angel silently waving goodbye.

Except for a hurried lunch break we didn't see much of each other for the rest of the day. While Angel was off sawing lumber, Luis and I dug holes for the building support posts. By nightfall I was beat. As I slumped against the side of the truck, Angel walked up and plopped down beside me, glistening with sweat and sawdust. A clean piney scent clung to her skin. If I kissed her she'd probably taste like it too.

She wiped an arm across her face. "So what's this neat thing I'm supposed to have? This morning you started to say I had a wonderful something-or-other but Uncle Bob grabbed you before you could finish."

"Oh, that," I said. "I was just going to –"

"Wait." She held up her hand. "Don't tell me. Let me guess. Now, you gotta tell the truth."

"I promise."

Angel scratched her head. "All right," she said. "Might as well start at the top. Could it be my hair?"

"No. That is, it's really pretty and all, but . . ."

"But just not wonderful, right?" She scratched her head. "Then, how about my eyes?"

"Nope."

"Nose?"

"Sorry."

She glanced down at her chest. "It sure as hell can't be these." Sheepishly I shook my head. Angel's breasts were really nice, but a little on the small side.

Finally she drew knees to her chest and wrapped her long arms around them. "Okay," she said. "Then what?"

I cleared my throat. "Uh, your voice."

"My *voice?*" She punched me in the shoulder. "God, what a freaking liar you are! You promised to tell me the truth!"

"I did, that is, I-I mean I am."

"But everyone says I sound like a boy!"

"Then they're not listening. *I* sound like a boy, uh, a man. But when you talk it's like . . ." I wracked my brain for what sounded right but as usual, came up short.

She crossed her arms, obviously suspicious by this time. "Yeah, like what, cowboy?"

"I guess it's kind of like . . . like when you crawl under a quilt on a winter night. A big, soft cozy one. The warmth soaks clean through your body and you want to stay there forever. I guess that's how it makes me feel."

She looked puzzled. "So you're saying it feels like you're sleeping with my voice?"

I groaned. "No, what I really mean is . . . oh God, I just wish I wasn't so lousy at explaining things."

Angel brushed the hair back from her face. "Actually

you're probably better at it than you think," she said. "You just do it a little different from anyone else I know."

The setting sun colored her cheeks like roses: roses covered with sawdust. She stretched and her shoulder brushed mine. I wanted so bad to be able to just take her hand and say something cool and romantic but as usual, the words just wouldn't come.

"So where are you staying?" I asked instead. "Out at the Motel 6 with the tourists?"

Angel pulled me to my feet and we walked behind the truck to where I saw a huge wall tent I hadn't noticed before. "This is home for the next few weeks," she said, "C'mon. Let me show you around *Casa Gallegos*."

The air in the tent smelled like kerosene and musty canvas. Three wooden cots stood half-hidden under rumpled sleeping bags. Sooty Coleman lanterns hung from the ceiling.

"The generator's for running the power tools," Angel said. "But Jimmy hates wasting fuel, so after sundown we fire these babies up." She touched the base of a lantern and it swung with a soft creak.

On a folding table in one corner, flickering red candles surrounded a picture in a golden frame. I stepped closer. "Is this Our Lady of Guadalupe?"

"That's Uncle Luis' traveling shrine. He takes it everywhere. Says *La Virgen* watches out for us." She pulled back a canvas partition. "And here's where I crash."

It was the closest I'd come to being invited into a girl's bedroom. Inside was a folding cot like the others and a battered suitcase lying open on the ground. Then I noticed a pair of blue cotton panties dangling from a thin clothesline. Angel noticed me notice, then pulled the panties off the line and casually tossed them on her sleeping bag with the rest of her clothes. Probably another sign I was too dumb to understand.

"And outside," she said, "is *el cuarto de baño*."

Now I'd been peeing in the woods my whole life but I'd never seen anything like this. Nestled behind a clump of sagebrush sat a plastic-lined bucket with a bright pink toilet seat on top. Copies of the *Hollywood Reporter* filled an orange crate next to the bucket and a roll of toilet paper fluttered from a nearby tree.

"That's it." Angel folded her arms. "So, what do you think?"

"Looks like the tent is pretty comfortable. But that thing," I said and nodded at the bucket, "is *truly* disgusting."

She grinned. "No argument there. But it's only for a few weeks. I guess I wouldn't mind so much if I could take a shower. We brought the stuff to build one and there's a stream downhill we could use for water. But everyone's too busy to help."

"Uh, then how 'bout we do it together? If you want to, that is."

Her face brightened. "You would? I mean, right now?"

"Sure, I'd love to –"

"Power down!" Through the trees I saw Bob next to the generator. "Power down!" he shouted again. "Ten seconds, everyone!"

We ran toward him. "No, wait!" Angel cried. "Uncle Bob, we're going to work on the shower!"

"Sorry, sweetheart." Bob killed the ignition and darkness rolled across the campsite like spilled ink. Lanterns flared beneath the tent. He pulled a flashlight from his pocket and handed it to Angel before walking away.

Frowning, she clicked on the light. "Like it would have killed him to wait a few minutes."

"Well, maybe we can do it tomorrow."

She grabbed my arm. "No way, José. First some chow then we get to work."

"Without power?"

"Damn straight," she said and pulled me back toward camp. "Where's your sense of adventure, cowboy?"

After a bowl or two of Luis' four-alarm chili, we hung lanterns in the trees and dragged lumber into the flickering pool of light.

"Can't tell you how much I appreciate this," Angel said as she opened a tool box. "I hate admitting I haven't showered for two days. Bet I'm a kinda stinky, huh?"

I held the flashlight as she measured and marked the boards. "I think you smell just, uh, fine."

She smiled. "And here I didn't think you noticed."

God, I notice everything about you. "No, I mean I kind of like the smell of sawdust."

"Yeah? Me too." She parked the pencil behind her ear. "What's your favorite kind?"

"Pine, I guess."

She nodded. "Pine, yeah. Pine is good. Spruce is nice too. Of course I really dig red cedar, but it reminds me of a hamster cage."

This was about the strangest conversation I'd ever had, but it was with Angel Suarez and right now that was all that mattered. "So where'd you learn so much about sawdust?" I asked, as she finished one board and started on another.

"In school, mostly." She nudged the toolbox with her foot. "Go on, have a look."

The box was made of polished wood with shiny brass hardware. It looked more like a piece of expensive furniture than a place to store tools. Inside a scribed oval on the lid were the words 'A. Suarez, Manual Arts High School' in delicately carved letters.

"This and a mahogany secretary desk got me an 'A' in Wood Shop." She picked up a twig then knelt to sketch in the dirt. "Okay, now here's how the shower goes together. Not too complicated but I figure it's good practice for building the sets."

"You mean you haven't done this before?"

She shook her head. "No, I've just been keeping the books for my uncles since I was fourteen. They got this little hole of an office over a *bodega* in East L.A. Pays okay but it's boring as hell. So this summer I talked Bob and Luis into letting me get my hands dirty. Jimmy didn't want any part of it so I've gotta prove myself if I ever want out of that stupid office again. Screw things up and it's *adios* and a one-way ticket back home."

"Then let's get this finished," I said. "Who knows, maybe he'll be easier to handle after a good shower."

Two hours later we were done. On top of the wooden framework we bolted a black-painted barrel surrounded by a silvery curved reflector. A length of hose with a sprinkler head dangled from one end of the barrel, pinched shut by a rusted clamp.

"Fill this baby in the morning," she said, patting the tank, "and by sundown the water's warm enough for a pretty decent shower."

"Neat," I said then stepped inside the framework and pretended to shampoo my hair. "But not very private, is it?"

"Don't worry," she said sweetly. "I brought a shower curtain." She handed me a fat black marker. "An artist always signs their work. I prefer a carving chisel but I guess this'll do for now."

Carefully I printed my name on the wood in large, bold letters then Angel added hers below mine. The black Ink feathered into the dry wood:

CODY HARRISON
Angel Suarez

"Hey, not bad," she said and slapped my back. "Not bad at all."

As we headed back to camp I glanced over my shoulder at the shower, silhouetted against the moonlit sky. Magic Markers on a two-by-four wasn't quite like carving your names in a tree, but it was a pretty good start.

After Jimmy's warning I set my alarm extra early and woke just before sunup. I tucked my arms under my pillow and stared up at the ceiling; once again it had been a wild and crazy night with Billy and his kin. This time we were driving the cattle across a wide, rain-swollen river. We were all soaked to the skin and once I even had to jump in after a calf taken by the current. Mama gave me a thank-you slurp when I showed up with her missing baby: a nice, wet cow kiss. Yawning, I crawled from bed and stood in the darkness, staring at my shadowy reflection in the dresser mirror and wondering what it all meant.

Before I left I looked in on Sam; she was snoring away as usual. At first I worried about leaving her alone till she reminded me there was a loaded shotgun by the back door and a rifle by the front, and she was pretty good with either one if need be. The Mondragon's house was only a couple hundred yards away too.

"And besides," she added, "this way there's less chance we'll kill each other before Mom gets back."

The sun had just cleared the mountains as I reached the set. Angel stood at the stove warming her hands and dashed over to my truck when she saw me. "What are you doing here?" she asked.

I tapped my watch. "Making up for being late yesterday," I said. "It's seven-thirty and you are my witness."

Angel put a finger to her lips and led me away from the tent. I didn't like the anxious look on her face. "Is something wrong?" I asked.

"No, just that I took your place on top of Jimmy's little list."

She turned away and leaned against the side of the truck as if the reason was written on her back for me to read. I stood it for ten whole seconds before I reached out and touched her shoulder.

"You're gonna think it sounds stupid," she said, turning back to face me. "But it's about last night when we were out."

Out? "What in the heck does that mean?"

Angel shrugged. "You know, out in the dark. Out away from camp. Out someplace where he couldn't keep his eye on me."

I didn't need to ask who *he* was. "I'm listening."

"Anyway," she continued, "he said it wasn't, you know, *proper*. I explained to him what we were doing but it didn't seem to make any difference."

"But that's crazy!"

She sighed. "No, that's Jimmy. You just don't get him."

I folded my arms. "Oh, yes I do. I was standing right there when he hit you."

"Hit me?"

"That first day, remember? All you were doing was catching up on some shut-eye when he whacked you with —"

"That?" Angel started to chuckle. "Look, he was just getting my attention. I probably deserved it too. But God, he'd never do anything to hurt me. Just put that out of your mind right now."

"Yeah, well, it still kind of bothered me."

She smiled at me and there was something in her eyes I couldn't quite read. "Look, I know Jimmy's a major pain sometimes," she said softly, "but I happen to love the crabby old guy." She fished a couple of plastic buckets from under the truck and handed me one. "I'll tell you why if you want to know. But first you've got to help me with something."

I wrinkled my nose. "Emptying the toilet?"

She laughed. "Filling the shower."

Angel ran on ahead of me and by the time I reached the creek she was sitting on a moss-covered boulder. She dipped a handful of water; droplets spilled through her cupped fingers. "God, it's so beautiful here," she said. "Back home the only things with water in them are the flood channels." She scooted over to make room and I sat down beside her. "Does it have a name?"

"No. Not officially, anyway. It's just a creek."

"No name, huh?"

She sounded disappointed but that's all it was, just an unnamed creek like dozens I'd fished, or swam in on so many hot summer days. But today *something* seemed different about it. The splashing water sounded almost musical, like a song without words. Willows drooped around us as if hiding secrets behind their sharply pointed leaves. Even the rocks looked like they'd been carved from polished granite and set there just for us to enjoy.

Angel gathered a handful of pebbles and tossed them one by one into the water. "Something this pretty really should have a name," she said. "You can't just call it a . . . a *creek*, like it isn't important or anything."

Her knee brushed mine. "Yeah," I agreed. "Not right at all."

"So let's name it," she said. "You're from around here. Come on, what should we call it?"

I thought hard, but all that came to mind was Suarez

Creek. "Uh, gee . . ."

"Oh, you're a big fat help." She stood and then her face suddenly brightened. "How about . . . Showerstall! That's what we're going to use it for, right? Yeah, good old Showerstall Creek. I like it. What do you think?"

"I couldn't do better myself."

Grinning, Angel plunged the buckets into the newly-christened creek.

Back at the shower she steadied me as I filled the barrel. It took a few trips but when the last bucket was empty I jumped to the ground and dried my hands on the back of my jeans. "Okay, now you can tell me about Jimmy."

She thought a moment. "Maybe tomorrow."

"What, after you made me carry all those buckets?" I said. "Come on, Angel, you owe me."

"Really? Since when do I owe you anything, cowboy?"

I jammed my hands in my pockets and stared at the ground, punishing a twig with my boot. What the heck was so secret?

"Now don't get all serious and stuff," she said. "Jimmy's just a little protective when it comes to me. See, some of the girls in the 'hood are either pregnant or they've already got a kid, maybe two. He just doesn't want it happening to me, that's all. I guess it's his way of saying he loves me."

I blinked. "You mean, he thought I was trying to –"

"Get in my pants?" she interrupted. "Probably. But he thinks that about every guy who gives me a second look. So when he found out I was hanging around after dark with this strange-looking Anglo boy . . ."

"Hey, I'm not a boy."

Angel smiled. "And you're not so strange-looking either." Without another word she leaned toward me. Our lips touched and then parted so fast I hardly knew what happened. First kisses usually said something, but not this one. It didn't even promise I'd get another. But in a weird sort of way that was what I liked. No promises. Endless *possibilities*.

Angel grabbed the empty buckets and we set off through the tall grass. From a distance I saw Jimmy sitting by himself, nursing a cup of coffee. Something told me I needed to fix things with him pronto but as I turned in his direction Angel stepped in front of me.

She put a hand on my chest. "And where do you think you're going?"

"To talk to Jimmy. You know, to set him right about what happened. I don't want him thinking that you and I were . . ."

"That we were what? Kissing?"

"No."

"Making out?"

"No! That is –"

"What, don't you want to?"

"Yes! I-I mean, no! Damn it, I just don't want him thinking those things about me." I looked into her dark eyes. "About, uh . . . *us*." As soon as I said that word I realized I was assuming a lot; for all I knew there was no 'us'. Even though she'd kissed me I didn't have a clue what it meant or even if it meant anything at all.

"Sounds like you're trying to protect my honor," she murmured, in a way that sounded both surprised and pleased. "Most guys I know hate dealing with Jimmy. You've seen what he's like. Soon as he gets all up in their face they take off like *el Diablo* was on their tail."

I folded my arms. "I'm not afraid of him."

She brushed the hair up off my forehead; her fingertips felt warm against my skin. "No, I don't suppose you are," she said. "But do yourself a favor and take it slow. Show up on time and do what you're told. Once he knows you better you can talk if you like." She tugged my arm. "Come on, it's almost eight."

Jimmy glanced at his watch as we walked into the tent. He caught my eye and nodded. Angel stole up behind me and handed over a mug of coffee. "That was probably as close as you'll get to a compliment," she whispered. "Better enjoy it."

Bob bustled into the tent. "*Buenos dias, niños.* Hope you two had a good sleep 'cause today's when the fun really starts."

He unrolled a set of sketches and some faded photographs, then described the movie version of old Furnace Creek. There would be two main buildings but they were just thin walls and roofs supported from the rear by heavy timbers. Sheds, privies, a wooden sidewalk and some canvas settlers' tents would complete the scene.

"Today we set the support posts," he said. "*Muy importante*. If it's not done right everything ends up crooked."

Angel leaned over the drawings and pointed. "Are those all eight-bys?"

"Eight by eight by twelves."

I whistled. Posts that size would be a flat-out pain to handle.

"They've gotta be set *perfectamente*," Luis said. "Jimmy's gonna run the mixer –"

"And cement ain't cheap," Jimmy interrupted, "so I don't want none of it wasted, hear?" He turned and walked away, muttering to himself.

Chuckling, Luis nodded after his brother. "That old mixer's one temperamental son of a gun. Only Jimmy can seem to make the damn thing work."

Bob fired up a cigarette. "Square and plumb," he said to Angel and me. "That's the key. Think you two can handle it?"

She elbowed me in the ribs. "No problem, right?"

"Sure." I didn't know what the all fuss was about. I'd

probably set hundreds of fence posts in my life. How different could this be?

Angel took charge. Once we loaded the pickup she drove while I shoved posts off at each hole. After we muscled them into place she levelled them up, bracing each with two-by-fours as I hauled cement from the clanking mixer. She really was amazing to watch; I'd never known anyone who seemed as self-confident as Angel Suarez. Of course I admired her body but I was fascinated by how she worked without a misplaced step or wasted motion. In a way it was strangely attractive.

Our eyes met and I looked quickly away. "Okay, I know you're not *staring*," she said, wiping the sweat from her face. "But what is it this time?"

"Uh, it's just that, well, you're really good with that . . . that hammer."

She shook her head. "You cowboys sure know how to impress a girl, don't you? First you like watching me work. Then I find out you want to sleep with my voice. Now it's 'gosh, ma'am, ya shore do swing a mean hammer, don't 'cha?'" Her drawl was so thick you could've buttered bread with it.

I felt my cheeks flush.

"And look, he blushes too," she said, grinning. "You really are kind of different."

"Different: bad or different: good?"

"Just *different*. Usually after a couple of days, most

guys are hanging all over me and feeding me a line of bullshit about how I'm the most beautiful girl they've ever seen." She pulled off her gloves. "So why aren't you?"

"I guess because you're not," I said without thinking.

She folded her arms. "How's that?"

Oh, God. "No, wait! I-I didn't mean —"

"Take it easy there, cowboy," she said. "We've got mirrors in my house too."

What I meant was that beautiful was more than just a pretty face but as usual it got screwed up in the translation. Maybe there was a short circuit in my brain.

"Besides," she added. "I don't trust guys who're too slick, especially when I know damn well they're lying. You're honest. That's better."

She scooped up a handful of nails and dropped them in a keg. "And it's kind of fun guessing what you'll say next. Like you'd die for a peek at my earlobes or maybe you think I've got these really terrific-looking, I don't know . . . feet."

I glanced at her boots. "Well, now that you mention it . . ."

She pointed the hammer right between my eyes. "Don't even go there, cowboy."

By the end of the day I swore I trudged twenty miles behind that stupid wheelbarrow. Finally Jimmy emptied the mixer, pouring the cement we needed to set the last post. But in my hurry to be done I lost my grip on the wheelbarrow handles and it overturned, spilling wet cement everywhere. Fortunately he hadn't seen what happened.

"That's great, just freaking great," Angel muttered as she surveyed the mess. "Now what do we do?"

"Simple," I said quickly. "If we move fast we can shovel most of the cement into the hole before it hardens. Then we toss in a few rocks to take up the space that's left. That's how we set fence posts anyway."

"I don't know . . ." Angel began. "It's not how Uncle Bob told us to do it."

"It's either that or we go back and beg Jimmy for more cement. I'm sure he wouldn't mind mixing us up a fresh batch, would he?"

She rolled her eyes. "Okay, but you better be right about this."

I picked up the shovel. "Rocks," I said. "Now go scare up some big ones."

Next day I began following Angel's advice about getting on Jimmy's good side. I showed up early and worked like a dog till quitting time in hopes he'd see what a decent guy I could be. Trouble was, I couldn't tell if it was working or not. So after three days, with work done and Angel off showering, I caught up with good ol' Uncle Jimmy for a little man-to-man talk.

He listened for a while with an eyebrow raised, then said "You want to take my niece to a *bar*?" He tapped a finger against his head. "Are you *loco en la cabeza*?"

"The Painted Lizard isn't a bar," I said, working to keep the nervousness out of my voice. "I mean, it is, but not on Wednesdays. See, that's when they have Family Night. Then there's pop and nachos and a band. No booze. Everyone just dances, hangs out and has themselves a good time."

"*La noche del familia.*" Bob looked up from his plans. "Now that sounds pretty safe to me. Besides, we can't keep Angel cooped up here all the time, Jimmy. She's still a kid, remember? It's not healthy."

Jimmy snorted. "Better than her riding around at all hours with someone we don't really know."

"Maybe Jimmy's right," Luis said. "What if the boy's secretly an axe murderer?"

"Or a car thief."

"Or a Protestant," Luis added.

I made a quick Sign of the Cross on my chest. Bob and Luis laughed but Jimmy just frowned. "Very funny."

"We won't be out late," I promised all of them. "I swear I'll have her back here by eleven o'clock. Sharp."

At last Jimmy threw in the towel. "Enough!" he said, then turned and pointed a finger right between my eyes. "I'll take a chance on you this time, boy. But by the Blessed Mother, if you're one minute late you'll live to regret it. *Comprende?*"

"*Absolutamente!*" I said and grudgingly he shook my outstretched hand.

Happy as all get out I doubled back towards Showerstall Creek, going over the plans again in my head. Tonight would be perfect. After dinner in a real restaurant, we'd take a long, slow drive to town. With any luck she'd slide over and sit beside me. What would happen next was anyone's guess. As I walked along the creek I remembered the first time we sat here side by side. So much had happened since then that it seemed like forever ago.

I saw the shower through the trees and was about to call her name when the plastic curtain parted and Angel stepped out. Her white robe made her look like one of those Greek goddesses we learned about in history class. She shook her hair and flying droplets made the briefest flash of a rainbow. As she stepped into her flip flops I noticed she really did have terrific-looking feet after all.

A twig snapped under my boot. Seeing me, she gasped and frowned. "And just how long have you been standing there?" She pulled the robe a little closer around her neck.

"Not long." I said, aware that only a layer of terrycloth separated me from a naked girl. "Just wanted to let you know I'll be back to pick you up in an hour."

Angel stared at me from beneath those thick eyebrows. "Come again?"

"Pick you up," I repeated. "First we'll go and get us some dinner, then –"

Shaking her head she pushed past me, furiously kicking pine cones out of her way. I followed with a sinking feeling in the pit of my stomach. "Uh, did I say something wrong here?"

"No, it's what you *didn't* say," she snapped. "You've

got a heck of a lot of nerve just assuming I'd say yes."

"But I already checked it out with Jimmy," I said weakly. "I thought, that is, I hoped you'd like to."

"That isn't the point," she said while finger-combing her hair. "Jimmy doesn't get to control everything I do. Why didn't you ask *me*?"

"Isn't that what I'm doing now?"

"Not even close. Asking is when you say 'Angel, would you like to go out with me?' It'd be nice if you'd actually consider *my* feelings before you go making plans."

I turned away, wishing I wasn't too old to cry but then she grabbed my shoulder. "Oh no, you don't," she said. "Not till we get this straightened out."

As our eyes met her mouth formed a sudden oval of surprise. "Wait . . . you were afraid I might say no, weren't you? Don't lie; I can see it in your eyes."

I squeezed my eyes shut and blurted out "Uh, would-you-like-to-go-out-with-me-tonight-Angel? Please?"

"Okay, okay," she said at last. "If only to see what's up with that crazy head of yours."

Forty-five minutes later I was dressed and back. Angel dashed out to meet me with her hair flying behind her. "This is about the best I can do," she said breathlessly. "Think I'll fit in?"

She wore boots, a denim skirt and white tank top, but what I noticed most was the band of tanned skin where those last two didn't quite meet. "Uh, you look really great," I said. Oh, she'd fit in all right; like a tiger in a room full of kittens.

As we got into the truck Angel tried to sit beside me but the busted springs in the seat made that impossible. Things went downhill from there. The *Ojo de Dios* café was closed – courtesy of the local health department – so we settled for greasy burgers and fries at the Dairy Treet. My so-called romantic drive ended when I ditched the truck to avoid a coyote that darted across the road. By the time we parked at the Painted Lizard I wondered what else could possibly go wrong.

Inside, the place was packed. Music blared from a country and western band set up on the polished oaken stage. There were so many bodies on the dance floor it was hard to breathe, let alone move.

"Jeez, you can hardly hear yourself think!" I shouted.

"Screw thinking!" She grabbed my hand. "Come on, let's do this, cowboy!"

Fortunately, line dances were pretty easy to learn, even for a guy like me with two left feet. We did the Boot Scoot and were starting the Electric Slide when I felt a tap on my shoulder. There stood Sam, grinning like a raccoon.

"What are you doing here?" I gasped.

"Same as you, O Big Bro. I hitched a ride with the Mondragon's."

Angel shouldered me aside. "Now, you've *got* to be

Sam. I've heard all about you."

"Is that so?" Sam eyed me suspiciously then turned to Angel. "Care to hit the little girl's room with me?" Angel flashed me an in-your-face grin and together they disappeared into the crowd.

I spent the next twenty minutes avoiding my friends and their dates, wondering what the heck Angel and Sam were up to. Anything was possible where my sister was concerned. Halfway through my third Mountain Dew a hand touched my shoulder and I heard "Let's get some air, cowboy."

Once we were outside, Angel sashayed down the street, snapping her fingers over her head. "Now *that* was cool," she said, grinning. "I never knew that old shit-kicking music was so good to dance to."

I caught up and took her elbow. "All right, what did she say?"

"Say? Who said we talked about anything?" she said innocently.

"Oh come on. You guys took darn near forever."

She shrugged. "There was this line. Yeah, that's it. We had to wait in a reeeeal long line."

"For twenty minutes?"

"Well, we washed our hands too. And besides, even if we did talk about anything – and I'm not saying we did – it was between Sam and me. If you're so curious why don't you just ask her?"

"'Cause I'm asking you."

She grinned and said "Tough," then bumped her hip against mine. Before I could say anything else she grabbed my hand and hauled me down the street to Carlisle's Antique Store.

"Wow, check it out." She pointed to a dust-covered end table in the front window. "See, that's what they call Mission style: the Arts and Crafts Movement. Isn't it beautiful?"

She rattled on about quarter-sawn oak, mortise-and-tenon joints and a bunch of other stuff I didn't quite get. I understood the dreamy look in her eyes, though. Would she ever look at me like that?

Holding hands, we wandered on down Ute Avenue, in and out of the yellow pools of streetlights. Sounds filled the night; dogs barked; crickets chirped in the sagebrush; a train whistle echoed on the far side of the valley. Everything was familiar, but somehow new and different. I'd spent a hundred nights in Furnace Creek but never with a girl like Angel by my side. It felt so good I wished it could last forever.

"So what's the big deal about an old table?" I asked her at last. "Didn't you say you wanted to do construction work?"

Angel shook her head. "Nah, this is just to earn some bucks. Someday I'm gonna have a studio of my own." She spread her arms wide. "Okay, picture this: *El*

Salon de Suarez. Custom furniture by yours truly. Cool, huh? My shop teacher thinks I've got a real eye for design."

She did; I remembered that beautiful tool chest. "Can you really make a living doing that?"

Angel leaned against a lamppost. "Who knows, but at least it'll be something I chose to do. That's what's really important, right?"

"Must be nice to know what you want to do with your life."

She shrugged. "Nothing's for certain but you gotta start somewhere. That's why I'm busting my hump here. Aside from the *dinero* this summer is a major waste of time."

"Is that so?" I said, hoping to sound a little offended.

"Sure. While all my friends are hanging out down at Venice Beach, I get to sleep in a tent, pee in a bucket and deal with the local cowboys." She smiled. "Okay, maybe that last part's not quite so bad."

"That's a relief," I said.

"And besides, once you get past that innocent face of yours you're a whole lot more complicated than you look. Take tonight for instance. Come on, you had to know I'd want to go out with you. I mean, we have kissed a few times."

"Uh, just once," I reminded her.

She flashed that mysterious smile again. "So far. But

just how certain do you have to be before taking a chance on something?"

I shrugged. "A written guarantee would be nice." I knew it sounded lame but after all I'd been through how else was I supposed to feel? Taking chances was Sam's thing, not mine.

Angel laughed, but in a way that said she understood.

"I guess I just want to know everything will be okay when the dust clears," I continued. "Not knowing what's going to happen kinda makes me nervous." We sat on the creaky bench by the hotel. "Is that weird?"

"Not really," she said. "When I turned fifteen I really wanted this guy to come to my *quinceañera:* Chad Herrera. Cute rear end, killer eyes. We're talking major babe. I really thought he liked me but I was scared to ask him until my *amigas* dared me. When I did – get this – the asshole laughed in my face. Right in front of everyone. How low is that? I wanted to crawl off and die, just freaking *die*."

"Now hold on a minute; that doesn't prove anything. You took a chance and you got slammed big time. Did that make you feel any better?"

"Maybe not that second, but sometimes that's what you gotta do. Sure it hurt, but least I didn't have to wonder about it anymore. I knew, and that was that."

That made no sense but as I started to protest Angel stood and pulled me to my feet. She snagged a lock of my hair and wrapped it around her finger. "You know, you worry too damn much," she said and draped an arm across my shoulder. "You talk too much too. Is that all your mouth is good for?"

Even I got a hint like that. I slipped my arms around her waist and pulled her close to me. We kissed a few times, longer and deeper than before. Then she lay her chin on my shoulder and whispered in my ear: "Still want that written guarantee?"

Sudden headlights caught us and the Mondragon's battered Suburban roared past, horn blaring. Carrie and my sister leaned out the back window. "Remember what I told you!" Sam called.

I glanced at Angel. "Was that for you or me?"

"Me, I think."

"Okay, then what did she mean?"

She frowned. "You're awfully nosy, but okay; maybe your name came up once or twice tonight." She twisted out of my arms and leaned against the driver's side door of my pickup. "And I don't see what the big deal is. It was just . . . stuff."

That's what worried me; Sam knew a lot more stuff than I cared to imagine. "Such as?"

"Oh, like where you go to school. That your favorite snack is a tortilla covered with – yuck – peanut butter." She wrinkled her nose. "Which is a waste of a good tortilla, by the way. And . . . do you really not know how to ride a bicycle?"

"Never had to; we always had horses."

"Figures. Let's see, what else? You sleep with your mouth open, wear briefs instead of boxers, and she might have mentioned your ex-girlfriend, Becca somebody or other."

Here it comes. "Becky Matthews," I said. Although we'd hung out together for a while last spring, I doubted she ever thought of herself as my *girlfriend*. In any case it ended with the usual 'it's not you, it's me' bullshit. And I hadn't told Sam a thing about it either; she probably saw it on Becky's Facebook page.

"Sam said she doesn't like her very much and thinks you could do a lot better." She grinned. "Which you obviously have, by the way. So anyway, she said this Becky broke up with you last month. You're not seeing anyone right now and that as far as she knows . . . you're still a virgin."

I was about to stammer "the hell I am!" when I paused. Although it was true, Sam couldn't have known. And even if she did I doubted she would say anything one way or the other. That left only one explanation; Angel was trying to find out for herself without being obvious about it.

"As if Sam would know," I said as casually as I could.

Angel gave me half a grin. "Okay, so maybe she didn't say that. She just warned me I'd better be nice to you. That's all, I swear." The streetlight caught her face in its pale yellow eye. "I guess I just was curious, so kill me."

"You could have asked, you know."

"Uh huh. And I suppose you'd have told me the truth, right?"

Like every other guy I'd probably have lied through my teeth. "Sure," I said, but all she did was roll her eyes.

We didn't talk much on the way back to camp. Angel rested her head against the back of the seat, humming quietly to herself. The night wind tugged at her hair while she gazed at the blur of fields and meadows, silent as the blue-white moon.

It was hard to concentrate on the road as I remembered the warmth of her arms around my neck and how it felt being with her, laughing, talking or just walking side by side. The kissing was getting a whole lot better too, but I didn't know if Angel was just being friendly or had something more in mind. And what was that bit about me being a virgin? Did it mean she was hoping for a guy with some experience or one with none at all? It was a little frustrating but I couldn't think of an easy way to find out.

We arrived back at the set with four minutes to spare. I turned off the engine and we sat listening to the *tick-tick-tick* of hot metal in the stillness.

"Thanks for taking me tonight," Angel said. "I had a super nice time. And you're a pretty good dancer too." She opened the door. "So I guess I'll see you tomorrow."

"Wait," I said before she could get out. "When we were back in town, uh, why did you want to know . . . *that* about me?"

She shrugged. "Like I told you, I feel better when I know where I stand. With anyone."

"But would it make a difference?"

Angel slid from the truck and closed the door. "Sleep tight," she said, and vanished into the darkness.

All summer I'd been remembering the strangest things, so when I headed to the set a few days later I wasn't surprised to be thinking about the cocoon I found when I was little. For a week I kept it in an empty mayonnaise jar on my dresser and checked it every day, wondering what was inside.

One morning the scabby brown sack split open. I yelled for Dad as a bright green insect – a Luna moth – fought its way out. As it hung motionless in the jar, limp and exhausted, I thought it was the most beautiful thing I'd ever seen.

"I-Is it dead?" I asked, my nose pressed to the glass.

"Open the jar," he said.

Heart pounding, I unscrewed the lid and blew gently into the jar. The moth roused itself, flexed its wings a couple of times and fluttered out my bedroom window, brushing my face as it passed.

"That's amazing!" I said.

Dad nodded. "It seems like a miracle to us," he said, ruffling my hair. "But it's just doing what it was born to do. No more, no less."

It sounded familiar. Everyone around me seemed to be working toward something. Angel polishing her woodworking skills, J.T. struggling to restart an acting career. Liebowitz, out to repay Billy by making this film. In a way I envied how they each had found something to work toward, something to guide them. As I pulled up and parked, I wondered what it was that *I'd* been born to do.

The tent flap parted and Angel stepped into the morning air. Her black hair was neatly brushed, gathered into a ponytail pulled through the back of her cap. She looked amazing. If living in a tent made you look that good maybe the whole world should go camping.

She stretched luxuriously, stifled a yawn and walked over to the hissing camp stove. "Wake up there, bright eyes," she said, as I ambled up.

"I'm awake. How about you?"

"Barely." Angel took a sip of coffee. A trickle escaped the corner of her mouth; she wiped it away and licked her fingers, delicate as a cat. "Oh, once I finally got to sleep things were fine," she said. "But getting there seemed to take forever. I never thought I'd miss hearing gunshots and sirens. But here . . ." She gestured toward the snow-capped mountains. "I've never been anywhere this *quiet*. Almost feels like we're at the end of the world."

"Not exactly," I said. "But sometimes you can see it from here."

She laughed. "Anyway, for a while I just lay on my cot and stared up at the tent roof. There were all these weird shapes moving around on the canvas. It kinda creeped me out till I realized it was the moon shining through the trees. Then I couldn't take my eyes off it."

"You should try sleeping outside sometime," I said. "First you unroll your bag beside the fire. Once the flames die down all you can see are stars. Millions. Billions, maybe. More than you could ever imagine in your life. And if there's no moon you can even make out the Milky Way, kind of like a fuzzy white band from horizon to horizon."

She smiled. "Wow. I'd really love to do that sometime. Back home you can't really see stars with all the streetlights. But what's the deal with *los perros*?"

"Dogs?"

"Uh huh. I was almost asleep when all this yapping and barking starts up. Don't you guys have some kind of a leash law around here?"

Talk about a city kid. "Those were coyotes," I said, watching her eyes widen. "When I was growing up, every now and then Dad and I would head up in the hills to watch the stars come out. Sometimes if the night was warm we'd stay out till morning. Just him and me. One night I remember he told me that every star was a coyote's spirit. And then he said when we hear coyotes howl, it doesn't mean they're lonely. They're just calling to their ancestors, asking for advice."

"That so?" She raised an eyebrow. "What kind of advice would that be?"

Dad never got around to actually explaining that part. "Whatever they need to know to get by, I guess. Like where to find food. Or water." I smiled. "Or maybe how to raid a henhouse and not get a tail full of buckshot."

Angel shook her head. "You are really something, you know that?"

"I am, huh?"

She nodded. "And I gotta tell you, that first day we met I figured you were kind of a . . . goof."

"Gee, thanks a lot."

"Yup, just your typical redneck; hat, boots and a whole lot of 'tude. But the more I'm around you the more I wonder if maybe I was wrong." She thought for a moment, chewing on her lip. "You're more like this . . . this old bookcase I bought at Goodwill."

Now *that* was just what every guy wanted to hear. "Keep going," I said slowly.

"Okay, stay with me. See, there in the store with all

the other junk it looked like a real project, but when I got it home it wasn't anything like what I expected. The joints were strong. It stood straight and tall – not even a tiny little wobble. Oh sure, it wasn't fancy but it had real character and the grain in the wood was absolutely amazing. All I had to do was buff it up to see how beautiful it was."

"So all I took was some polishing?"

Angel smiled. "Guess that's one way to look at it," she said and squeezed my hand. "But maybe I only helped uncover something that was there all along."

We spent that day and the rest of the week working on the two false-fronted buildings. It was almost like assembling giant 3-D jigsaw puzzles. First we laid out sheets of plywood then nailed on a thin veneer of rough-cut planks. After mounting the windows, we guys held each section up against the support posts while Angel fastened it with a nail gun.

Then Luis went to work. With only a hand saw he fitted the sections together, overlapping random boards here and there so the seams wouldn't show. Once we added a false roof you swore it was a real building not just a shell a couple of inches thick.

Every day we worked sunup to sundown no matter the weather. It was pretty tiring but I'd never had so much fun. And all the while I found myself surrounded by feelings and memories I forgot I ever had, like the Luna moth and the stars and coyotes.

It had been that way all summer too: talking about buffalo with J.T.; remembering those trail rides with Dad and my first time on a horse; even all those dreams as Billy McAllister, whatever the heck that meant. In a strange way it was almost like I'd found a hidden part of myself that made me feel more alive than I had in years. But was it going to last? I sure wanted it to, but right now, the jury was still out on that one.

On the last day of June I arrived a little late for our regular night out. "About time you got here," Angel said. She hopped in the truck then slid over and kissed me, making me extra thankful I'd fixed the broken seat. "So what kept you?"

Her lips were damp and soapy-tasting. "Just getting some stuff ready for tonight," I said.

She gave me a look. "Exactly what kind of stuff are we talking about here?"

"Be patient. It's a surprise."

I drove us through town and up into the pine-scented foothills. We bounced in and out of the deep, weathered ruts that had once passed for a road. House lights grew few and far between then disappeared altogether. And all the while Angel sat quietly beside me, staring at the passing trees. She hadn't talked much since we left but I figured she was just bushed from work.

As the sun dipped below the horizon I parked the

truck in the middle of a broad meadow, hemmed in by towering fir trees. Bats fluttered noiselessly overhead, chasing insects in the cool, silent air.

"Now what?" she asked.

I took her hand and we walked around to the back of the truck. "Climb on in," I said and dropped the tailgate. She settled into the pile of fresh hay I loaded before leaving home.

"Is *this* your surprise?" she asked, leaning up on one elbow. Her voice sounded cool and strangely distant.

"Nope." I fished a grocery bag from under the hay and handed it to her. "This is." She hesitated. "Go on, take it. It won't bite."

Gingerly, Angel unfolded the top of the bag and peeked inside. Her nose wrinkled. "Cookies?"

I nodded. "Chocolate chip. Sam baked 'em for us this afternoon. Pretty nice of her, huh? I've got a thermos full of hot chocolate too. I made that myself: Dad's old recipe." I leaned close to her ear. "Don't tell a soul, but the secret ingredient is cinnamon."

Angel shook her head. "I'll be damned," she said quietly. "Cookies. Hot chocolate."

"Something wrong?"

"No," she said. "I guess it's . . . it's just not what I expected."

"Which would be . . . ?"

She took a deep breath. "A six-pack of Bud."

I stared at her, vaguely aware my mouth was hanging open. Great. It sounded like Angel expected a guy who could score some brew and who shows up but sweet little Cody Harrison, complete with snacks.

Angel sighed. "Look," she said, "so maybe that was what I expected. I didn't say it was what I wanted. It's just that it's happened to me before, see? First, the guy pulls out the *cervesa*. Then he's all like 'hey girl, just one beer, okay?' and before you know it he's on top of you trying to unzip your jeans."

So that was it. Frustrated, I folded my arms. "Come on, that's not fair, Angel. Why would you think I'd do that to you? And besides," I reminded her, "it's not like we haven't kissed before."

"No, but that was different."

"How?"

"Because then it was *my* idea. *I* kissed you, remember? It's okay when I get to call the shots but when the guy makes a move I guess I get a little, well, freaked. Maybe that's why I hassled you at the shower." She smiled. "Hard feeling in control when you're only wearing a bathrobe."

A week ago I would have let things go at that, maybe even laughed it off like it really didn't matter. But not tonight. I'd never cared for anyone the way I did with Angel and although I didn't want to start an argument, maybe it was time I stopped pretending I didn't have feelings too. After all, she was the one who said I had character; maybe it was time I showed her a little of it.

"No offense," I said, "but I think you've been listening to Jimmy too much. I know maybe *he* would figure that's what I wanted but that's no reason you should. What, are you afraid being out here with me?"

"Of course not." She sounded defensive. "You should know that by now."

"Okay, then *be* with me, Angel. You can't use Jimmy as an excuse to push people away."

She twisted a strand of hair around her finger. "Isn't that how you use your dad?"

I frowned, "What's that supposed to mean?"

"Something your sister told me," Angel said quickly. "That night when we were hanging out at the Painted Lizard, remember? Sam said that she's scared how much you changed after he died. How you've just sort of given up on everything and everyone, including yourself." She chewed on her lip. "I think maybe I see a little of it too."

God, would my sister ever learn when to shut up? "Sam's just a kid," I snapped. "She thinks she's so smart but she doesn't know everything."

"She knows you, doesn't she?"

I practically shouted "Nobody knows me!"

"And whose fault is that?" Angel said, her voice rising. "Look, I'm sorry your father's dead. Really sorry, okay? I can't imagine how awful I'd feel if it was my Dad.

But what has it been, almost five years? Sam seems to have found a way to deal with it. How long before you do?"

"That's my business. And why do *you* care all of a sudden?"

Her eyes flashed. "Because . . . because that's what girlfriends do, damn it!"

"Oh yeah? Then maybe you . . . uh . . ." My voice trailed off as the words sunk in. I'd never been real clear on how a girl friend became a *girlfriend*. Now it just happened right in front of my face and in the middle of an argument too. I was so confused that I just stared, hoping she'd be the one to speak first before I screwed things up again.

Angel sighed then took my hands in hers. "You know, I've really gotten to like you. A lot. At first I wasn't sure why. Let's face it, we are kind of different, aren't we?"

I gave her a weak smile. "Maybe just a little."

"That's what was so weird. See, I couldn't put my finger on anything special you did or said, and then it hit me: it's just the way you make me *feel* when we're together. Like you . . . you really understand me." She rubbed my palms, slowly warming my skin beneath her fingers. "I guess I felt kind of safe with you too, that you'd never do anything hurt me. But then tonight when you drove me all the way up here and plopped me down in a bed of hay – *hay* for Christ's sake – I was afraid I had it all wrong."

"But Angel . . ."

She raised her hand. "No, let me finish. And then when you pulled out that bag I thought for sure you were going to turn out like every other jerk guy I've ever been with. That everything I'd thought about you would turn out to be just another lie I'd made up to fool myself. But then that didn't happen. I guess what I'm trying to say is that really meant a lot to me, more than you know." Then Angel took my hand and pressed it against her lips. "And so do you, Cody."

It was the first time she'd ever actually spoken my first name and hearing it in that wonderful voice was more than I could have hoped for.

We sat silently for a while just holding hands until Angel said "I guess that was our first real fight, huh?"

"I guess so." I turned and looked into her eyes. "And I'm sorry if I –"

"Don't apologize," she said. "I'm the one who didn't have any right talking about you and your Dad."

If she really was my girlfriend, maybe she had *every* right. And besides, what if it was true? Jimmy. My Dad. Were we each using them to avoid getting hurt again? I couldn't answer for Angel but the thought of it made me uneasy.

"Say, I'm getting a little cold here," she said, rubbing her bare shoulders. "Wanna break out that hot chocolate?"

I pulled out the thermos and poured us some. Angel took a sip. "Hey, this *is* good," she said, then helped herself to a cookie and handed one to me. "But I gotta know; if you didn't plan to make out, how come you brought me all the way up here anyway?"

"Just to look at the stars," I said, nodding up at the sky, which was growing steadily darker.

"Why?"

"Well, you once told me that you wanted to." I took a slow, deep breath. "And besides, maybe that's what . . . boyfriends do." I gently slid my hand behind her neck and around her shoulder, then drew her into a kiss that was better than every other kiss in my entire life, times about ten.

We settled down side by side. Hay crackled under our bodies. I put my arms around her and she lay her head on my chest like it was the most natural thing in the world. As she snuggled closer I felt the soft, deliberate beat of her heart. Had my father ever imagined me like this, lying under the night sky with a girl like Angel in my arms? Somehow, I thought he just might have after all.

"Do you know you're the only guy who's ever given me cookies?" she whispered and laid her arm across my stomach.

"Now, why doesn't that surprise me?"

Above us, the first stars twinkled to life in the deep,

indigo sky; for a whole lot of reasons I knew it was going to be a beautiful night.

"Coyotes, huh?" she said.

"Yup. Every last one."

"This is *so* insane, Cody." Teeth chattering, Sam cradled a section of gutter in her arms. "Nobody'd believe I'm standing on the roof at six in the morning," she said. "In the freaking rain, too."

"Put a sock in it okay? We're almost finished." I tightened the last bolt on the new downspout and we climbed back in through the bathroom window. "Really appreciate your help, Sam. That's needed fixing for the longest time."

"No doubt." She grabbed a towel and started to dry her damp hair. "But why have you been so busy the past couple of weeks? I mean, painting the porch, cleaning out the hayloft, patching the tool shed roof. It's not like you."

"That a problem?"

She grinned. "Naw, I'm beginning to think I like the

new and improved Cody Harrison. But seriously," she continued, "what happened? Finally planning to rejoin the human race?"

Maybe I was. J.T. may have gotten the ball rolling, but ever since my starlight talk with Angel I'd been thinking – I mean, *really* thinking – about where my life was going. I didn't have any answers yet but at least I had started to ask myself some uncomfortable but important questions.

We went downstairs to the kitchen where Sam grabbed a bowl and a box of Froot Loops. "I'm waiting," she said as she opened the milk.

"Guess I'm not really sure." I filled the coffee pot and plugged it in. "But maybe after all this time I finally ran out of excuses, Sam."

As I opened the refrigerator door a pair of arms curled around my waist and squeezed. "I love you, Cody," my sister said. "You know that?"

I caught her in an affectionate headlock. "Yeah," I said as I knuckled her scalp. "I love you too."

It was raining a little harder when I got to the set; if this kept up maybe we should think about starting an ark next. As usual, Jimmy was about as cheerful as the weather. "Someone was here last night," he said. "I went out to take a piss and I saw this . . . this shadow sneaking around. I'm sure of it."

Angel and I exchanged here-we-go-again looks. I'd

never met a guy like Jimmy in my whole life. No matter how well work was going he always managed to find something to fret about. Maybe it was what made him happy.

Bob pushed his blueprints aside. "*Dios mio*," he said, rubbing his eyes. "The Mercantile's already up and finished. *Los niños* will have the hotel trimmed out by this afternoon. We're ahead of schedule and now you're starting to imagine things."

"Imagine, nothing," Jimmy snapped. "I know what I saw. I told you it was a mistake getting mixed up with Liebowitz again. Remember what happened on *Coronado's Children?*"

"That's right," Angel said between sips of coffee. "Didn't you catch a bunch of guys creeping around the set one night?"

"Get it right, girl," said Bob. "There was just that one *hombre*. Lebowitz' backers hired him to check on us, just to make sure things were moving along. Once he saw everything was okay he left. End of story."

Jimmy snorted. "Hah! You know damn well he was there to make sure they weren't getting screwed over!"

I hated even thinking what I said next: "Uh, you're not telling me Liebowitz is sort of . . . sketchy?"

"No." Bob turned to me. "Now old Ben might be a lot of things but not that. Sure, he practically runs his company on pocket change but that's nothing new. The guy's known for making a dime in the budget look like a dollar on the screen. So sometimes he cuts a few corners but it always seems to work out. It will this time too. You'll see."

That sounded a little better. As her uncles turned away Angel took my hand. "Time's wasting," she said. "Hasta la move-your-butt."

Angel walked on ahead while I paused for a moment to check out what we'd accomplished over the last few weeks. Like Bob said, the Mercantile store was ready to go. I glanced behind the front wall at the tangle of braces and beams that held it up, hardly able to believe it wasn't a real building. Once the hotel was completed we'd add some hitching posts, a board sidewalk, a couple of privies and rows of tents to complete the rest of the town.

By the time I caught up with Angel she had already propped an extension ladder against the two-story Grand Imperial Hotel. A lot of the action would be filmed here and I felt kind of proud Bob had left it for us to finish.

"How about I hand the stuff up and you nail?" said Angel. "You've got longer arms."

"Fine with me," I replied and climbed to the top of the rain-slickened ladder.

One by one Angel passed up the precut strips and I nailed them in place as far as I could reach on either side. The work was easy but kind of boring, so I soon found my mind wandering again. This summer had turned out a lot different from what I expected. I had myself a new job, a girlfriend – if you could believe it – and maybe even the start of a different way to look at life. Thinking back, I realized it all began that first day I saw those buffalo clouds in the western sky.

The drizzle continued while I fitted and fastened the trim pieces up under the eaves. Every so often I glanced down at Angel and watched the rain slicken her hair, bead on her cheeks. My stomach twitched a little from the height, but just thinking about the two of us – together, I mean – well, that did it too. It was kind of a strange feeling. Was I falling in love? I wasn't quite sure but just the possibility of it felt totally amazing.

By late afternoon we were just about done. "I think we'd better move the ladder over," Angel called up one last time. "Ground's getting kind of mushy here. I don't want you to fall."

"What, you won't catch me?" She laughed but when I straightened up I suddenly felt the ladder shift beneath me. "Angel!" I shouted, fighting to keep my balance. "Hold it steady!"

"I can't, damn it! It's sinking in the mud!" She threw her weight against the ladder but it kept tipping. My stomach twisted as I felt my grip on the ladder loosening.

"Bob! Jimmy!" she yelled. "Help me!"

Walls buckled around me and I heard the sickening sound of tearing wood. I grabbed desperately at one side of the balcony, lost my balance and fell. Flailing wildly, I hit the muddy ground with a loud *whuff*. Angel grabbed me under the arms and dragged me to safety just as a section of wall crashed right where I landed.

"Oh God," she cried as she cradled my head in her lap. "Cody, talk to me!" Tears glistened in her dark eyes but all I could do was nod.

The Gallegos brothers raced up. Bob and Luis bent over me while Jimmy pounded a fist against his thigh. "You gonna tell me I'm imagining this too?" he shouted.

"How is he?" Bob asked, ignoring his brother.

"Okay, I think," Angel said. "Probably just got the wind knocked out of him."

He whistled. "Now that is one lucky little gringo."

I started to shiver and Luis put an arm under my shoulder. "Come on, let's get him inside before he catches pneumonia."

Together they helped me into the tent. While Angel looked away Bob stripped off my wet clothes, wrapped me in blankets and laid me out on a cot. "Push the coffee into him," he said and then ducked back outside into the downpour.

Between the coffee and Angel's hand on my forehead I began to feel a little better. Physically, anyway. "Jesus, what happened?" I groaned, rubbing mud from my eyes.

"I'm not sure I know," she said. "It all went down so

quickly I couldn't see what caused it. But you don't suppose it was . . ." Her voice trailed off as Bob walked in from the rain, running fingers through his dripping hair.

"Now that is about the strangest thing I ever saw," he said. "One of the main support posts pulled right out of the ground. All this damn rain must have loosened the cement so it couldn't hold any more. First time for everything, I guess."

Oh shit. I opened my mouth to fess up but out of the corner of my eye I caught sight of Angel. She put a finger to her lips and slowly shook her head.

"At least it broke pretty clean," Luis added, "so we'll be able to re-use most of the wood. Gonna have to rebuild the balcony though; it's busted all to hell. Good thing we're ahead of schedule."

Jimmy scowled. "*Were* ahead of schedule."

"Don't worry about him," Bob said as he sat on the edge of the cot. "I was planning to send you and Angel to town for more supplies anyway." He lit a cigarette and took a deep pull. "I'll just add the extra stuff we'll need. Once this weather clears up a day or so will put us back on track again."

Luis laid a hand on my shoulder. "Listen, you've been shook up pretty good, so I want Angel to drive you home tonight."

I wasn't hurt that bad. "But –"

"No buts, amigo," Bob said. "Luis is right. Get yourself a good rest and she'll pick you up tomorrow on the way to town. *Comprende?*"

"*Si,*" I replied weakly. "*Hasta mañana.*"

After getting into some dry clothes I borrowed from Luis I climbed painfully into the truck. "We both know it was my fault, Angel," I mumbled as I settled into the seat. "Why didn't you want me to tell them?"

Angel leaned over and pulled the seat belt across my chest. "And what good would that do? Whatever happened, happened. Explaining why wouldn't change anything, would it? Besides, you were just trying to keep us out of Jimmy's way, that's all."

"Yeah, but I should have known better."

"Me too." She gave my shoulder a gentle squeeze. "But trust me, things will look a whole lot different tomorrow."

Angel returned early the next morning to pick me up. "Man, you must have been hurt worse than I thought," she said. "You look like hell."

"Actually I'm feeling better," I said as I climbed into the truck. "I guess I just had a lousy sleep."

"Lousy, as in 'nightmare'?"

"As in *major* nightmare."

"I used to have 'em all the time too," she said and pulled onto the highway. "Especially after my first trip to Sea World. I really loved watching the killer whales but then I used to dream Shamu was hiding in the bathtub drain, waiting to eat my toes."

I slumped in my seat. "That's cute, but I'm not a little kid, Angel."

"Doesn't make any difference. Everyone has nightmares now and then." She laid a comforting hand on my thigh. "So, are you going to sit there and make us both miserable or you gonna talk about it?"

Ever since Sam's brush-off I'd been dying to tell someone – *anyone* – what I'd been going through every night, but I still hesitated, worried what she might think. "It's kind of a long story."

She pushed hair back from her face. "And it's a long way to town. Besides, in *mi familia* nobody ignores their dreams. That includes me, Cody."

After a little more coaxing I told Angel all about my nightly dream-rides as Billy McAllister. I described the blazing sun and choking dust and our meals around the campfire, cactus and coyotes, lightning and rattlesnakes, everything I could remember. It felt kind of good to get it off my chest, but telling it to someone else made it seem more real, more vivid and in a way, more frightening. The only thing I didn't mention was the part about Tonka. Heck, I was still trying to figure that one out myself.

Angel coasted through a stop sign, barely missing an oncoming semi. "I think I understand why this is happening to you."

"I sure wish I did."

"Well, you said your Dad told you this story when you were a kid, right? Maybe this movie business has just sort of, I don't know, helped you remember some things you already knew. From there, it's not a big stretch to think you'd dream about it too, is it?"

As reasonable as that sounded I knew it wasn't that simple, not by a long shot. "Up until yesterday that might have explained it," I said, "but what happened last night was different, Angel. See, we were just bedding down the herd when we got ambushed. There were these four men on horseback and they came at us out of nowhere. I-I heard a gunshot and saw Pa fall from the saddle. And then there was the blood . . ." I swallowed. "Blood all over his chest."

"It's still only a memory," she said. "A bad one for sure, but what else could it be?"

I took a deep breath. "But see, that's the problem. When Dad told it to me he never went into all of the gory details. I was still pretty young and I guess he didn't want to spook me. So really I shouldn't have known what happened but somehow I did. And then —"

"There's more?"

I nodded. "Then I got shot too. Here." I touched a finger to my shoulder just above the collarbone, half expecting it to come away bloody. "When it happened my horse threw me and took off. God, it hurt so bad I thought I was going to die. Then they killed my uncles; shot them down one by one. I-It was horrible."

I glanced over at Angel. She stared straight ahead, fingers drumming the steering wheel. "So you still think it's just something I heard when I was a kid?"

Angel shook her head. "Not any more. See, it's not just what you're saying but the *way* you're saying it. Did you hear yourself? *Pa. I* got shot. *My* uncles. You weren't telling me about what happened to Billy anymore. You were telling what happened to you."

Goose bumps prickled my arms as I realized she was right. Somehow this had become *my* story too.

"God, I wish my Grandma Inez was here," Angel said, turning to me. "She knows how to interpret dreams. It's sort of a family gift. I don't have it – the gift, I mean – but I've learned enough to know you don't mess around with things like this; dreams, that is. She says they can tell us stuff about ourselves we may not even realize we know. About our past, what's happening to us now." She rubbed the back of her neck. "Or maybe even what's going to happen."

I was pretty sure I didn't like the sound of that.

"Promise you'll tell me if you have this dream again," she said. "I'd really like to know."

Nodding, I turned to watch the passing fields. There was one last thing but it rattled me so much I couldn't even bring myself to repeat it. As I lay there bleeding in the dirt I overheard two of the rustlers arguing over what to do about me.

"I say we kill him and be done with it," growled a deep voice, rumbling like an avalanche. "One bullet. We end it now."

"No," said another. "There weren't supposed to be no killing, Boone. You swore to it. Now I'll be damned if I'm going to finish this boy or let you do it neither. We're all knocking on th' gates of Hell as it is."

"Then leave him," said the first. "He'll be dead as the rest by morning."

Through a pain-wracked mist I heard them ride off, driving our cattle before them. Soon there was nothing left but silence and the echoes of that terrible voice: *kill him . . . kill him . . . kill him . . .*

A tour bus roared past on its way down to Mesa Verde. The day was warming up but I felt cold and miserable inside. Was it me or Billy McAllister doing the shivering? Even after a summer in his skin I wasn't quite sure anymore.

Once we got to town Angel dropped me at the lumber yard and headed off for some groceries. Inside the cluttered office Mr. Carlson scanned Bob's list of supplies then shook his head. "Afraid I can't help you, Cody."

Before I could ask why not, he pulled a thick ledger out from under the counter.

"And the reason," he said, "is that I've not yet been

paid for all of what's owed." He polished his glasses, set them on his pointed nose then ran a finger down the pages. "Let's see . . . yes, here it is. The first delivery of materials was ten thousand, eight hundred and sixty-six dollars. Five thousand of that was paid in advance, but as for the rest, well, Mr. Liebowitz hasn't even bothered to return my phone calls."

Damn it, Ben. "Come on, Mr. C.," I said. "I'm pretty sure they're filming down around Gallup this week. I guess he just hasn't had time to get a check cut."

"That's unfortunate." He put the ledger away. "Because until he finds the time, he won't get another thing from me."

My mind raced. I was the one responsible for the accident at the set; no way could I go back there empty handed. All that mattered now was getting those supplies. My stupidity had gotten us into this mess; my brains had to get us out.

"Now hold on," I said. "Suppose . . . I signed for it? What's still owed and everything else we need on the list. The T Bar S has a line of credit here, right?"

He nodded. "Of course."

"And my Mom gave permission for me to sign for whatever we needed, didn't she?"

"Yes, but I'm not sure this is what she had in mind."

I stood as tall as I could and looked him in the eye, man to man. "All I know is we've got to have this stuff,

Mr. C. Every bit of it. Today. I'm sure he'll make good on it. I-I trust him."

My stammering voice and sweaty palms said otherwise but what choice did I have? My point – and maybe even my whole future – was riding on getting this right. Despite C's in math, even I knew that one per cent of nothing was nothing.

Mr. Carlson stroked his chin for what seemed like forever as he mulled things over. "All right," he said at last, "but I doubt your mother would approve." He lowered his voice. "And I'm sure your father wouldn't if he was here."

I swallowed nervously; he probably had that one right. "But he's not," I said and held out my hand. "So just give me the pen, okay?"

A hand shook my shoulder. "Cody, wake up! Wake *up!*"

When I opened my eyes I was sprawled on the living room couch. Again. On the TV some guy was pushing a new and improved hemorrhoid cream.

Sam stared down at me with her arms folded. "Keep this up and we'll be able to rent out your room."

Groaning, I rubbed my eyes. These past few nights my dreams had gotten more and more intense. Burying the bodies of my kin under piles of rocks, unable to even mark their graves. Riding across the sagebrush, clutching my bloody shoulder, half-dead from pain and thirst. I was getting so freaked out that I'd been trying to keep myself awake, afraid to even close my eyes. But even I knew I couldn't watch TV forever.

Stretching, I asked Sam what time it was. She glanced at her watch. "Nearly ten-thirty."

My eyes snapped wide. Grabbing my boots I snatched up the Pop Tart Sam held out for me and dashed for the door. In the three days since the wall collapsed we'd repaired all of the damage but being late was bound to land me smack on Jimmy's shit list again.

When I got to the set their pickup truck was gone. Strangely, the place seemed deserted too. Under the work tent Angel sat on a battered ice chest doing her nails. Instead of work boots and overalls she wore sneakers, faded cutoffs and a flowered tank top.

She looked up and frowned at my rumpled outfit. "Oh Cody, did you sleep in your clothes again?"

"No," I replied, "this is my new look. Like it?"

Angel laughed. "Not really, but at least I'm getting used to it. And how come you're late?"

"It's a long story." I looked around. "So where is everybody?"

"Gambling," she said as she fanned her nails. "They decided to take a day off to hit that Indian casino over in Cortez. Luis loves the blackjack tables. Jimmy and Bob pull slots. And they all like to drink. They'll probably be back late too."

"Really?"

"'Course, I had to promise Jimmy we'd stick around and keep an eye on things." She stood and grinned. "So let's get a move on."

"But I thought you said –"

"I know, but come on, nothing's going to happen. Besides, I'd really like to spend some free time with you in the daylight." She patted the cooler. "I made us a picnic too."

A day all alone with Angel was more than I dreamed I'd ever get. Quickly I stowed the cooler in the bed of the truck. "So where do you want to go?"

"Your wheels, your choice," she said. "Surprise me."

I opened the door for her. "You mean Angel Suarez is gonna trust a guy to make the first move?"

"First time for everything," she said and whacked me on the rear end. "Just don't push your luck."

A half-hour later we stopped at a crest in the road, overlooking a valley that was ringed with red-rock cliffs and tall fir trees. In the distance, water splashed over mossy boulders and flowed out across a lush green meadow sprinkled with purple wildflowers.

I leaned on the wheel. "Recognize it?" I asked.

Angel shook her head. "A little help."

"Hot chocolate and cookies."

"*Dios mio*," she said, nose pressed to the glass. "I never realized it was this pretty."

After parking the truck we walked through the trees to an outcrop high above the valley. I felt my heart beat just a little faster; in the daylight it was even more beautiful than I remembered. While we made our way down the trail to the valley bottom I told Angel about our plans to raise buffalo here. Although I hadn't thought about it in years, everything seemed so clear that it was almost as if Dad was standing right here, going over those ideas with me again.

"For starters, you gotta remember that buffalo don't exactly like being penned in," I told her, "and when you weigh a couple thousand pounds, fences just aren't enough. But here there's only the one access road in; all we have to do is block it off and they can't get out. It couldn't be easier."

As we walked through the meadow I showed her the thick, sweet grasses that carpeted the valley floor; acres and acres of perfect grazing. We stared up at the tall granite cliffs that would provide protection from driving winter blizzards. Finally we knelt by a bubbling spring; the one thing that would make it all possible. I took her hand and dipped it beneath the water.

She looked up in surprise. "It's warm."

I nodded. "It's a thermal spring; the only one for miles around. See, it feeds that little pond over there. It's only about eighty degrees but when we'd come up here — even in the middle of winter — it's always ice-free."

Angel reached over and dried her hands on the back of my jeans. "Hot and cold running water, huh?"

I nodded. "Yup. Everything here in one place.

There's nothing like it within a hundred miles, shoot, maybe nothing like it in all of Colorado. It was going to be perfect but then . . ." I glanced at Angel. Her dark eyes were fixed on me. "Okay, now what are *you* staring at?" I asked.

"You." Smiling, she draped an arm around my shoulders. "That is, it was you, but in a way it wasn't. There was this . . . this *look* on your face that I've never seen before. Your voice was different too, almost like you were speaking straight from your heart. Guess you're really into this buffalo thing, aren't you?" We kissed and she gently squeezed the back of my neck. "Does that make sense?"

"Maybe it's the same way you feel about *El Salon de Suarez*." I whispered in her ear.

"So you understood that?"

"Yeah." *Now more than ever, Angel.* My insides gurgled and I rubbed my stomach. "Uh, did I hear something about a picnic?"

I spread a blanket out on the ground near the pond while she unpacked the cooler. It was quite a feast; chorizo sandwiches, Fritos and salsa, some fruit and a six pack of Coke. For an hour we talked and ate, feeding each other drippy orange slices and exchanging long, slow kisses after each one. It felt wonderful to be with her and like Angel guessed, just being in the valley gave me a strange sense of possibility.

After we finished eating Angel yawned and stretched out on the blanket. She slipped off her sneakers and wiggled those perfect toes. Then I lay beside her, face down on the warm scratchy wool. She put an arm across my waist then slowly worked her hand up and under my t-shirt, gently massaging the small of my back. No girl had ever done that to me. I wanted it to go on forever but the warm sun, a full stomach and too many sleepless nights weighed heavy on my eyelids.

"Okay, I've never actually had a guy fall asleep on me," said Angel, soft and close to my ear. "But I'll make an exception this time. Take yourself a *siesta* now, but I want you wide awake when we get back to the tent, understand?"

"Sure," I said, and let my eyelids fall. As she snuggled close to my side I felt her top brush against me, smooth and tight as a second skin. A second skin of flowers.

"Will he live, Father?"

Two brown-robed figures stood together at a nearby window, their backs to the bed where I lay. The taller one shook its head. I didn't know much Spanish lingo but enough that I could figure out what I heard next.

"It is truly a miracle he made his way here," he whispered. "We have done all that we can. Come, let us say an *Ave* for him." Heads bowed, they left the room and closed the door softly behind them.

I took a deep breath, knowing at last I was safe. I had

seen the Mission bell tower from afar and turned my horse toward the whitewashed adobe walls, hoping to find someone to help me. As I rode into the open courtyard I practically fell from the saddle and into the arms of the surprised Franciscans.

Slowly, I sat up in bed. Although my shoulder still pained me it was freshly bandaged; the hurt still there, but not as sharp. My head throbbed again and I lay back down. Somehow, I was still alive; alive and alone. But what now? Was I to slink back to town like a whipped pup? How could I tell them all about Pa's death, the killing of my uncles, the loss of our cattle? Truth was, I couldn't; I would sooner have died myself.

Through a narrow window I glimpsed my horse, tethered to a hitching post. Had I not found him after the ambush, right now I'd be as cold and dead as Pa and his brothers. I needed to get help and pronto, but the nearest law was in Santa Fe, near a hundred miles south and in another territory to boot. No, if justice was to be had it would be up to me to deliver it.

Next to the bed, Pa's Henry rifle lay propped against a stool; the gunmen had overlooked it after they killed him. I brought it with me hoping that one day I could make them all pay for what they'd done. As I touched the cold steel barrel I heard that deadly voice again, those horrible words echoing in my head: *"Leave him. He'll be dead as the rest by morning."*

Trembling, I squeezed my eyes shut, unable to hold back the tears that spilled down my face. With fists clenched at my side I swore an oath right then and there, a promise to the souls of my murdered kin. I would find a way bring the herd home. I would make things right or die trying.

Above me a wooden crucifix hung on the wall. Our Blessed Savior nailed to a cross: bloody yet triumphant. I closed my eyes and prayed for the strength I knew I would need.

And I prayed I would not fail my family again.

Drops of rain splashed across my face and when I opened my eyes I saw Angel standing over me. "Come on, Cody," she said, helping me to my feet, "better run before we get soaked."

As we hiked back to the truck Angel asked if I had dreamed about Billy again. I started to answer but decided against it. Billy McAllister might have taken over my nights but I'd be damned if he was going spoil my day alone with Angel.

Once we were on the road back to camp Angel unbuckled her seat belt and stretched out on the seat, something she hadn't done since the first day we met. Then it was her feet in my lap; now her head lay on my thigh, her long black hair spilling out across my jeans.

Angel smiled up at me. "You know, you've got pretty eyes for a guy." She reached up and touched my chin.

"And Sam was right," she added. "You really do sleep with your mouth open. It's kind of cute."

I kissed her hand, then she took mine and laid it across her stomach. When we got back to camp we would probably have hours alone before her uncles returned. Who knew what would happen then? The possibilities seemed endless. Well, almost endless. The box of condoms I bought last year sat unopened at the bottom of my sock drawer, so I guessed sex was out. Like that was going to happen anyway. Still, the thought of everything that *could* made me press a little harder on the gas.

As we neared the last curve before camp I noticed a car parked beside the road, almost hidden by some chokecherry bushes. That was a little strange. Aside from our usual comings and goings I hadn't seen anybody else this far out in the boonies.

I slowed and then pulled in behind it for a closer look. The black SUV with tinted windows and California plates stirred an uneasy feeling down in the pit of my stomach.

"Angel," I said and turned off the engine. "Check it out. I think we may have company."

Thunder rumbled as she sat up beside me. "Who do you suppose it is?"

Jimmy's warning about guys sneaking around the set now seemed a little too real for comfort. "I don't know but if they parked all the way back here it means they didn't want to be seen. They must think we're all gone."

She tightened her fingers around my arm. "Cody, what should we do?" There was a flicker of fear in her voice.

With her uncles out of the picture there was no way to avoid getting involved. "I don't guess we've got a choice." I quietly opened the door. "Just stay behind me and keep low till we figure out what they're up to."

A light drizzle wet our shoulders as we crept through the underbrush with Angel holding tight to my belt. My mouth was paper-dry and I felt my heart race as we got closer. Once we made it to the tent I peeked carefully around one corner, holding my breath. Not fifty feet away stood a short man dressed in black from head to toe. He held what looked like a burning road flare. As I watched in horror he casually tossed it through the front door of the hotel, which erupted in snake-like coils of orange flame.

"Stay here!" I yelled then ran toward the fire. Waves of heat scorched my face. The smoke half-blinded me and I covered my mouth, barely able to breathe. At the last moment the short man caught sight of me. He turned to run but I lunged at him, grabbed the bottom of his jacket and dragged him to the ground.

"You ... son ... of ... a ... *bitch!*" I yelled, slamming my fists against his back, over and over. He covered his head and let out a bloodcurdling shriek.

A thick arm slipped around my neck and jerked me off my feet. As I struggled a knee dug into my lower back and a bolt of pain shot up my spine.

"Goddammit, Eddie," a voice growled close by my ear. "You said this place was deserted. Where'd this little shit come from?"

The other man staggered to his feet. "Damned if I know," he said, rubbing his shoulder, "but if he's here then that little Mexican bitch is probably around too."

Windows shattered in the hotel and I saw flames eating away at the Mercantile too. I squirmed in the vice-like grip, scarcely able to breathe.

"And take it easy on him," he added, "we ain't got orders to hurt —"

I heard a wet thud and the arm around my neck went suddenly limp. A heavyset man fell at my feet, hands pressed to his head as blood gushed between his sausage-like fingers. Through blurry eyes I saw Angel silhouetted against the flames, swinging a thick branch of wood like a baseball bat.

Eddie grabbed at her shoulder. "Don't touch her!" I yelled, then pushed her out of the way and swung at him with all my strength. His eyes grew wide and my fist hit the bridge of his nose with a satisfying crunch. Bone snapped beneath my knuckles and he staggered back, bleating like a sheep.

Something struck the back of my head. Stars whirled

in my brain and I dropped to my knees in the mud. I tried to stand but couldn't regain my feet.

Lightning flashed. Thunder roared. And then darkness swallowed me.

I was only out for a couple of minutes. Once I regained consciousness Angel and I huddled miserably under rain-soaked blankets and watched the fire burn itself out, helpless to do anything. Luckily the downpour kept the flames from spreading; just a few more feet and we'd have lost the tents, all of the equipment and probably half the national forest. Maybe even our lives too. As the last flames flickered out, a sickening, drowned-campfire stench hung heavy in the air; a smell I knew I'd never be able to shake.

By the time Angel's uncles returned it was well past dark. Once they saw there was nothing to be done they had Angel drive me down to the Circle K to find a pay phone. First I called Sam and filled her in, telling her to stay at the Mondragon's tonight. Then after a few tries I managed to get a hold of Liebowitz down in New Mexico. If I expected him to explode at hearing the news I was wrong; he listened without asking so much as a single question. All he said to me was "Do nothing. I'll be there tomorrow."

As I hung up the phone I told Angel it was almost like he was expecting the call.

Someone must have overheard me at the Circle K because next morning Sheriff Ruiz arrived to see what was left of the set. It wasn't much; the hotel and mercantile were nothing but mounds of wet, blackened wood. Only some hitching rails and the wooden boardwalk had escaped the flames.

Liebowitz showed a few hours later. As he took in the damage he wiped a handkerchief back and forth across his sweat-beaded forehead. "My God," he said softly, over and over. "My God."

The sheriff picked up a charred piece of lumber and held it to my nose. I sniffed, recognizing a familiar scent. "Gasoline?"

"Cheap, fast and efficient." he said, then dropped the wood and dusted off his hands. "And also very easy to detect. Most arsonists try to hide their tracks but I think this one was sending a message." He shot Liebowitz a sidelong glance. "Any idea who might want to do that, sir?"

To my surprise the producer nodded slowly. "My

business associates, no doubt."

"Thought as much," the sheriff said. "Well, I'm gonna poke around a mite longer then we'll need to have us a little talk, Mr. Liebowitz."

As Angel kicked at the remains of a broken window Jimmy shook his head. "I warned you all," he said to nobody in particular. "But not a damn one of you wanted to listen."

Ever since that first burst of flame I'd been moving around in a fog, like this was all just a another bad dream that would soon be over. As the truth began to sink in, the afternoon sun felt suddenly hot and close. Lightheaded, my knees started to buckle till Luis caught and steadied me.

Sheriff Ruiz gently parted the hair on the side of my head. I winced and pulled away at the bright stab of pain. "Son," he said, "has Doc Peters seen to this here lump?"

"Not yet." Angel put her hand under my arm. "But I'll take him."

Together we stumbled toward the truck with Angel supporting me on one side and Luis on the other. Liebowitz walked ahead of us, his hands clasped behind his back.

"Your 'business associates'?" I said loudly. "Just what the hell does that mean, Ben?"

He sighed. "It means you should never use the same property as collateral for two different loans. I tried a little creative financing to fix my cash flow problem but I guess Lazarri and Chen compared notes and didn't like what they saw."

"Wait, a minute," said Angel as she eased me down on the pickup's seat. "You're saying the guys who loaned you the money, they set the fire?"

Liebowitz nodded. "Their muscle did."

"But that doesn't make any sense."

He shrugged. "You wouldn't think so, but gentlemen of their standing have a certain, shall we say, reputation to protect. When someone crosses them, bad things tend to happen."

Now that everything seemed clear I said what I should have said weeks ago: "Ben, I'm done and this time I mean it. Nothing is worth this kind of grief. Forget the point. Forget everything, okay? Just pay off Mr. Carlson and we're quits." Then I filled him in on what happened, from the spilled cement to my signature in the lumber yard account book.

As he listened a pained look crept across his face. "I'm afraid that presents a problem," he said. "Like I told you at the beginning, it's all a matter of cash flow. That means I pay the most pressing bills and hold the others – like your friend Carlson – till later. Once we wrap, I cash out my production bond and pay them off too. It usually works out just fine." He glanced at the smoldering ruins. "But now with all this . . ."

Blood pounded in my ears; this was fast becoming another nightmare. "Oh come on, you've gotta have some kind of . . . of insurance, don't you?"

"Of course, but arson is a crime. A claim like that takes months to settle. Investigations, reports, they'll probably even want to talk to Señor Sheriff over there." He rubbed the back of his neck. "I can't wait that long. If I don't find a way to wrap in the next two weeks I'll be in so deep I won't ever get out. And trust me, some of my other backers make those two look like Mother Teresa."

I struggled to my feet, gripping the door handle for support. "And so where does that leave me, Ben?" I shouted. "On the hook for five thousand dollars?"

"Now don't you go making that my problem, kid," he said curtly. "Signing for those supplies was your idea. If you'd just tried to call –"

Angel stepped between us and gently settled me down on the seat. "*You* sit," she said to me, then turned and poked Liebowitz in the chest. "And *you* be quiet. The two of you can fight about this later but we're going to the doctor, *now.*"

Eyes down, Liebowitz nodded then turned and walked slowly toward Sheriff Ruiz who was waiting for him with folded arms.

"*Jesu y Maria,*" Angel said as she fired up the truck. "Cody, you should have told me you signed for all that stuff. Why did you do it?"

I sighed and rested my head against the rear window. "Because of what we talked about at the Painted Lizard."

"We? What the heck did *I* say?"

"Don't you remember? All that stuff about me being too afraid to take chances. I figured that seeing as the whole mess was my fault I had to try and find some way to get us out of it. Since it looked like that was the only chance I was going to get, I took it."

Angel shook her head. "But I was just talking about dating and stuff, not signing your life away."

"I know, I know, but in a way it all made sense to me, Angel. And then remember that night I drove us up to look at the stars? What you said about my Dad got me to wondering who really was to blame for my screwed-up life. I thought about it a lot." I folded my arms. "I guess maybe that was part of it too."

"Okay, so what are you going to do now?" she asked, drumming her fingers on the steering wheel. "Slink back to town like a whipped pup?"

I turned and stared at her. "What did you say?"

Angel frowned. "I said 'sit tight and see what the sheriff turns up'."

"Oh, right," I replied, turning away. "I guess that's what I'll do." But maybe I had just heard exactly what I needed to hear.

As we neared the Furnace Creek turnoff the sun

crept from behind plump gray clouds and washed across my face. Through the windshield a wall of jagged peaks filled the western sky, clean and fresh after last night's rain. For a moment they almost seemed to be beckoning to me, and just like that I knew what I had to do.

"Uh, go straight, here," I said as Angel slowed for the turnoff.

"Why?" She glanced at me. "Town's to the left, isn't it?"

"We're not going to town."

"But Cody, I promised the sheriff –"

"Look, I've had my bell rung before. Doc will shine a light in my eyes, have me stand on one foot and touch my nose to check my balance. Then he'll tell me to take it easy for a couple of days, so why waste the fifty bucks? I just want to go home, Angel." I touched her shoulder. "Please."

Sam met us at the front door and together they helped me up the narrow stairs to my room. I flopped down on my bed and let Angel tug off my boots while Sam draped the faded chenille bedspread over me. "Try and get some rest," she said as she lowered the shades.

Angel smoothed my hair and kissed me on the cheek. "Yeah, we'll figure this all out later."

I listened to their footsteps as they went downstairs. A few minutes later the front door opened and soon I heard the *creak-creak-creak* of the front porch swing and the murmur of voices. Quietly I gathered up my boots and crept downstairs to the kitchen. This time I didn't really care what they were talking about as long as it kept their attention off me.

After grabbing a few supplies from the pantry I pulled on my boots and a jacket then slipped out the back door, closing it softly behind me. I managed to make it to the barn unseen and was almost done saddling Zack when I heard a voice behind me.

"Your sister said I might find you in here," Angel said as she walked through the open doorway. "Maybe she does know you after all."

Thanks a lot, Sam. "Listen, it's not what it looks like," I said as she came closer. "I'm not running away from things. It's just that I've got to —"

Angel pressed a finger to my lips. "There's an old brick culvert behind my house," she said. "Used to be some kind of storm drain, I guess. Anyway, it's dark and cool and quiet inside. When I can't figure things out I just go and sit there a while. Usually it helps." Her arms circled my waist. "What I'm saying is that sometimes being alone is the only way to hear what's inside you."

I put my arms over hers and pulled her close to me. "I love you, Angel," I said. "God, I think I love you more than anything."

"I know," she whispered in my hair. "And I love you too, Cody."

We stood together and kissed, long and slow and deep while sparrows chirped in the eaves above our heads. At last I rested my chin on her shoulder and buried my face in her hair. I'd never said or heard those three words before, not with someone like Angel. It wasn't fair that I had to leave but now there really was no turning back.

Just then Zack put his nose against Angel's back and shoved. She laughed and then scratched behind his ears. "Do you think this is such a good idea?" she asked. "After you getting knocked cold and all."

"Probably not," I said as I tightened the latigo under Zack's belly. "But a cousin of mine once rode ten miles with a bullet in his shoulder. Reckon a little bump shouldn't slow me down."

"And how's your hand? You throw a pretty wicked punch, you know."

When I glanced down at my knuckles I saw a dried smear of blood – Eddie's blood – still on them. "Believe it or not," I said, flexing my fingers. "That's about the only part of me that doesn't hurt."

Angel smiled and looked at me like I was the hero in one of those action movies. She nodded toward the open doorway. "So exactly what do you think you'll find out there?"

I climbed into the saddle. "Not sure I know," I said, gathering up the reins. "But I remember Dad saying you could always find the answer if you rode long enough. Guess I'll find out if that's true."

"Guess you will." she said. "Oh, I also told Bob I may be gone for a while so I'll hang out here with Sam till you get back."

"Thanks. Just don't listen to anything she says about me."

"I promise. And you damn well better take care of yourself, Cody Harrison. *Vaya con Dios.*"

She stood on tiptoe and I leaned down for a final, lingering kiss. God, I'd have given anything to stay here with Angel Suarez but I knew if I didn't leave now I never would. Without looking back I pressed my heels against Zack's sides and we headed out of the barn and up towards the looming hills.

We rode up the old logging road behind our ranch then headed far out along the ridge that overlooked the valley. In the distance Tohachi Creek sparkled in the sunlight, water tumbling over huge mossy boulders. I stopped for a breath of air to clear my head. Once I got my bearings we followed the abandoned railroad grade for a mile or so then forded a little creek. From there it took only a few minutes to reach tree line.

The path wound deep into the forest. Now and then I felt a flicker of recognition at things we passed: a lightning-blasted spruce, pointing like a bony finger at the sky; small ponds surrounded with leafy clumps of willows; even a pair of squat gray rocks that resembled sleeping camels. Familiar, but nothing I could really put my finger on.

As the afternoon dragged on the trail branched so many times I pretty much lost track of where we were going. I felt a little lightheaded too; maybe I should have gone to see Doc after all. But what really bothered me was Angel's question; what *was* I hoping to find up here? Sure, it had all sounded pretty cool when I explained what I was up to, kind of like a knight riding off on a quest. And I loved seeing that look of admiration in her eyes. Trouble was, Dad never explained exactly what happened on those little trips of his. When I asked, all he ever said was "The secret is to expect nothing. Just leave yourself open and you'll find what you need."

Like *that* was a big help.

After a couple more hours we broke into the open just long enough to catch a glimpse of the setting sun, an orange ball in a blood-red sky. Not long after, a crescent moon crept above the trees, a grove of white-barked aspen, their slender trunks shrouded by evening mist. Aspen usually meant water nearby and sure enough I soon found a small stream. Zack drank gratefully while I gathered wood for the night.

Above us the summer constellations filled the sky: Cygnus, the swan; the mighty hunter, Orion, with his glowing belt of stars; and of course the Great Bear – Dad never called it the Big Dipper – almost directly overhead. As I kindled a fire I heard coyotes seeking advice from those cold white stars. Maybe I should try howling too.

After tethering Zack, I wolfed the can of Spaghetti-O's I'd set near the flames then wrapped myself in the saddle blanket and stretched out on the ground. A log snapped and sparks filled the sky, chasing themselves to cinders. It was eerily quiet; even the crickets seemed to have turned in early.

Miles away, Angel and Sam were probably getting ready for bed. Somehow I knew Angel would stay in my room tonight. Maybe she'd pull on one of my t-shirts before crawling beneath the sheets and laying her cheek on my pillow. Would she whisper my name before drifting off to sleep? I missed her so bad it hurt, but I had to trust in what she told me: *sometimes, being alone is the only way to hear what's inside you.*

Yawning, I pulled the blanket over my head and stared at the dying flames, too worn out to care.

16

"You're burnin' th' damn rabbit, Billy."

Jake Carlson took the wooden spit from my hands. "Didn't nobody ever learn you t' cook?"

He and Patrick Morrissey hunkered down beside me, next to the fire. "Now, we all swore t' help you," Pat said good-naturedly. "But we ain't about t' starve doin' it."

"Sorry," I said, but my mind wasn't on cooking no rabbit. For the best part of a week we'd taken stock of the rustlers, watching their every move to figure how we could best take them. Tonight, with no moon in the sky it was now or never.

I walked to my saddle and fetched Pa's rifle, the one he carried at Chickamauga during the war. The rustlers overlooked it when they killed him. I loaded the magazine and levered a bullet into the chamber. I'd bagged me just about every wild critter there was but I'd never shot at nothing that could shoot back. Truth be told, I was plenty scared; scared I'd get us all killed.

While those two tended to the rabbit, Lucius Pritchett stood all by his lonesome, his skin as black as the night sky. I'd come across him first. The night after I left the Mission I bedded down in his family's hayloft, only to wake next morning with his shotgun stuck in my face. It took some pretty fast talking but once he decided not to shoot me he agreed to help. What's more, he even roped Jake and Pat into it too. They were all three a year or so older'n me, chock full of piss and vinegar, bored with farm life and eager for a little adventure, I supposed. Me, well, I had other reasons.

"Hey Billy, Lucius." Jake held up the spit. "Want some?"

Lucius wandered over but I just shook my head and watched the three of them pick at that small pitiful carcass. *Sweet merciful Jesus*, I prayed, *let none of us die tonight*.

After letting them eat I walked back to the fire. Their eyes fell on me, waiting. "I reckon it's time," I said. "Let's go."

Lucius and I mounted up while the others followed afoot, leading their horses. Quietly we snuck down the arroyo to where the outlaws lay drunk and senseless around a roaring fire. The rough edges of my wound tugged at my shirt. I whispered a prayer of thanks to the

Brothers who'd took me in and stitched me up. Now here I was, leading a pack of boys into what might be the fight of our lives. By morning I might have killed a man, maybe even been killed myself. What would the good Brothers think of me then?

A twig snapped. One of the men sat up and stared into the darkness. We held our breath as he staggered into the bushes, scratching at his crotch. Only when he returned and started snoring did we dare move again.

The plan was simple. Our stolen beeves lay bedded at the mouth of a large alkali wash. Jake and Pat would circle round and spook the herd from behind. Then Lucius and I would swoop in on horseback, hoping to take the men before they got their wits about them: alive, if possible, dead if need be.

Had I my druthers I'd see them dance at the end of a good stout rope for what they'd done. Failing that I was more than willing to kill them myself, every man Jack of 'em. I swallowed nervously. *Should I die tonight, would I go to hell for wanting such a thing?*

As usual the men were careless and set no watch. While the others moved into position Lucius and I stood side by side in the darkness.

"Sure's hell hope this works," he mumbled through his cupped hands.

"Reckon that makes two of us."

A gunshot split the night. Cattle lowed nervously as

moonlight glinted on their massive horns. Almost as one the herd started to move. Our mounts whinnied nervously and we had to hold them in check as the ground trembled beneath us.

"Now!" I yelled and we spurred our horses, rifles in hand and bellowing at the top of our lungs. Suddenly sober, the rustlers snatched up guns and dashed to their horses. One of them loosed a blind pistol shot. A thunderous blast – Jake's shotgun, surely – and the man fell bloody and twitching.

Whooping like Apaches we pounded up the draw, dodging in and out of the panicky steers. The three remaining men had mounted up, desperately seeking a way through the milling cattle. In the firelight I caught sight of Jake.

"Help Pat," I yelled. "Round up the strays best you can, then stay put till we can send help back!"

"What, and let them get away?"

I patted the Henry. "Leave them to us."

"Well good luck," he shouted, then urged his horse into the darkness, calling Pat's name so he wouldn't get shot himself.

Together Lucius and I rode toward the pale dawn, hard on the heels of the fleeing rustlers. The hills were familiar and I realized we were nearer Furnace Creek than I'd thought. Three, maybe four miles was all. Close, but not enough for anyone to ride to our aid. For better or worse we were on our own.

Presently the men turned up the narrow creek bed where Pa and I had fished during the spring. Our luck was holding; with only one way in or out of the gulch it was the perfect spot to spring an ambush on *them*.

I gestured to Lucius and we dismounted and led our horses uphill. Soon we made the high ground above the creek and then crawled to the edge of the cliff on our bellies. Below, the outlaws stood by their horses, staring behind themselves as if Old Scratch himself was on their tail. I was mighty glad they didn't suspect we were just a couple of boys.

As Lucius aimed his rifle I touched his shoulder. "Remember," I whispered, "no killin' lest we have to."

He shrugged my hand away and fired a round just above their heads. "Drop 'em!" he yelled, but instead the men scrambled for their horses, shooting wildly in our direction.

A ricochet hit a boulder by my head and splattered grit in my face. Beside me Lucius squeezed off shot after shot. By the time I cleared my eyes the men were gone, leaving only dust and one of their own: a body face down in the creek, staining the water red.

My stomach churned. I'd seen corpses before but only after the undertaker had prettied 'em all up. For the second time in as many hours I'd seen sudden, bloody death. Gagging, I knelt and vomited my guts onto the cold red earth. When I was all puked out Lucius helped me to my feet. Shamed by my weakness, I looked away, afraid of what he would say. Instead, he pressed the Henry into my trembling hands.

"Ma allus' said there ain't no shame in bein' scairt," he said, resting a hand on my shoulder. "'Specially if'n it keeps you from gettin' yourself kilt."

Nodding, I wiped my mouth. Two dead. Would others die before sunup? Would I?

The men doubled back out of the mouth of the canyon and by the time we caught up with them they were headed straight for Furnace Creek. As we topped a rise the sound of gunfire peppered the air. A woman screamed and I suddenly realized we'd just driven a pair of desperate men into a sleeping town. Black-hearted, evil men who'd already killed and would doubtless kill again to save their stinking hides.

"Split up!" shouted Lucius.

I broke right, weaving my horse through the rows of white canvas tents. People staggered out, rubbing sleep from their eyes. I came within a hair of trampling a barefooted girl crying for her mother. More gunshots drew me to the Grand Imperial Hotel; they must be holed up there. I slid from my horse and edged along the side of the Mercantile to where Lucius was crouched, clutching his rifle to his chest.

He pointed at the hotel's second floor balcony. "I

think they be up there," he whispered. As if in answer a bullet splintered wood above our heads, driving us back.

By this time other men had gathered around us, guns drawn. Grinning, Lucius slapped me on the shoulder and said "this here's our fight, ain't it, Billy?"

Before I could answer he plunged headlong into the street, seeking better cover. A rifle cracked; he clutched at his leg and tumbled to the ground.

"Lucius!" I cried and ran towards him.

Bullets dogged my heels. As I knelt beside him I heard that hated voice, full of surprise and rage: "It's that goddamn kid! Kill him! *KILL HIM!*"

I swung my rifle toward the words and fired; a man staggered and crashed backwards through a plate-glass window. As I levered in a fresh cartridge I felt something explode against my ribs. Stunned, I flew backward onto the dirt.

Shouting erupted all around me, the voices of folks I knew and loved. Guns blazed then fell silent. The stink of gun smoke filled my nose. I struggled to get up but my legs wouldn't move. When I put a hand to my chest I felt a sticky warmth on my fingers.

Hands touched my forehead as a girl knelt beside me. It was Sarah, youngest of the Murdoch family. She was my first love. Why, she'd even let me steal a kiss from her before I left for Santa Fe.

"Oh, Billy," she whispered and smoothed my hair.

"Please God, no."

She took my hand and held it between hers. I felt calm, peaceful-like: everything was going to be all right. Justice had been done. I had made it back to my family and the herd would be coming home too.

High above me a flock of crows flew across the sky, wings flapping slowly. I heard one of them caw. The sun was hot but I shivered. And Lord, all I wanted to do was sleep. I managed to smile as I looked into Sarah's eyes, pale and blue as robin's eggs.

"Don't you worry none," I said. "I-It don't really hurt."

Above the fog-shrouded trees the eastern sky shaded from grey to pink. Shivering, I sat up and pulled the blanket tight around me, cold and hungry but most of all, mad. Standing, I kicked angrily at the dirt. "That's it?" I yelled as loud as I could. "Are you *KIDDING* me?"

Ears raised, Zack looked up in alarm but I was too pissed off to care. I'd spent practically every night this whole summer in Billy's head, following him to the bitter end and for what? Not a damn thing. Now he was dead and gone, leaving me no closer to understanding what any of this meant. What a total idiot I'd been to think that just riding up here would show me anything.

I rubbed my sleep-clogged eyes. I guessed Dad had it wrong; sometimes there just aren't any answers, no matter how long you ride. But then who could I blame but myself?

After drowning the campfire I packed what little gear I had and mounted up. "Come on Zack," I said miserably. Maybe I would have to slink back like a whipped pup after all.

When we stopped last night it was well after dark so I wasn't sure how to even start back home. As I wondered which way to go I caught sight of something at the edge of my vision. It lasted only a second but enough for me to see it was huge and brown, lumbering along like a . . . *buffalo?*

Hair rose on the back of my neck. Jesus, had I just seen Tonka, my stuffed toy again? I glanced behind me but saw nothing except the trail leading into the aspen grove. Without thinking, I turned Zack and headed that way.

After a little while we broke out of the aspen and rode into a broad, sunlit meadow, sparkling and dewy from the night before. In the distance I saw the gray shapes of buildings; one had a row of windows along one side. There was also a taller structure with a balcony, overlooking what must have been the main street of whatever town this used to be.

I swallowed nervously; now those I had *definitely* seen before. As we rode closer I was able to make out the faded words on top of the taller building:

GR ND IMPE IAL OTEL

"Son of a bitch," I whispered. Somehow through all this running around I'd found my way to what remained of old Furnace Creek!

After dismounting I tied Zach to a weathered hitching rail. No wonder things seemed familiar; it looked exactly like what we'd been building all summer, a set that was now nothing but blackened ash.

I pushed against the side of the hotel; it was in surprisingly good shape and I wondered if maybe, just maybe Liebowitz might be able to use the real thing instead. Although it could solve a lot of problems for everyone, was *that* the reason I'd ended up here? It didn't seem likely; besides, that strange dream about Tonka happened long before we'd run into trouble.

I felt a sudden chill as if someone was watching me. I spun round and found myself looking at the front window, broken pieces of glass dangling from its frame. No one was there but I still felt something hidden. Hidden, but not exactly hiding. More like . . .

Waiting.

Slowly I stepped inside the hotel lobby, waving tangled cobwebs out of my way and testing the weathered floorboards with each step. No sense ending up in the basement if I could help it.

The room was about twenty feet square, littered with

bits of yellowed newspaper and shards of glass that crunched under my boots. I took a deep breath. The air smelled old and musty but the room was empty. Just what – or who – had I expected to find here anyway?

A muscle twitched in the small of my back. Groaning, I put my hands on my hips and bent over backwards, stretching until my joints popped. When I opened my eyes I saw some letters carved into a wooden beam far above my head. I squinted and they swam slowly into focus:

It took every scrap of willpower I had – and then some – not to run terrified into the street. Instead I just stared, scarcely breathing. There was no doubt I'd carved those letters – shoot, I even recognized the way I made my D's – but God, when? And how the heck did they get up there; ten feet off the floor in a place I'd never been before? None of it made any sense and the more I struggled to understand the more confused I got.

Then I heard Dad's voice: *Expect nothing. Leave yourself open.*

Still shaken, I sat cross-legged on the floor then closed my eyes and forced myself to breathe long and deep. At first I heard only the dull rush of blood in my ears but once that faded there were echoes of a voice, growing louder and clearer till I recognized Billy's final words: *It don't really hurt.*

Unsure what that could mean, I waited a minute to see if there might be more, something I could better wrap my arms around, but that was all. With nothing else to go on, I finally put my head in my hands and repeated those words over and over as slowly and deliberately as I possibly could: "It don't really hurt . . . it don't really hurt . . . it . . . don't . . . really . . . hurt . . ."

It felt strange and maybe even a little embarrassing too, sitting on the floor in a tumbledown building in the middle of nowhere, chanting like somebody in one of those weird religious cults. What would Angel think if she saw me like this? Frustrated, I was about to give it up when before I realized what was happening, I was a twelve year old kid again, running eagerly through rain-slickened leaves.

Hey, Dad!

A rifle lay cradled in my arms. Dad's 30.06, the one he finally let me use.

You gotta come see this!

A herd of elk grazed down in the valley, out of earshot beyond the aspen grove.

Must be a hundred of 'em, Dad!

He raised his arms, waved, shouted at me.

Running, running, running . . .

My boots caught a half-rotten log. I fell, dropped the

rifle, heard it fire . . . And when I looked up he was there, sprawled on the ground in front of me. A dark stain crept across the front of his green flannel shirt.

Panicked, I slipped my hands beneath his shoulders. Although he was easily twice my weight I managed to drag him back inside the old hotel, out of the cold drizzle. I dashed outside to fetch saddle blankets and returned to find him propped against a wall, legs twisted in front of him like one of Sam's busted dolls.

He rubbed his thigh. "Can't seem to move these old sticks of mine," he said, as if it was just a plain old charley-horse that would go away in a minute.

I knew better, Kneeling, I tucked the blankets tightly around him. "Dad," I blubbered. "Oh, Jesus, Dad. I-I'm so sorry . . . if I hadn't been –"

"Stop." He put his hand on the back of my neck and looked straight into my eyes. "Now you listen here," he said. "It's nobody's fault, son. Bad luck it was, nothing more. You've got to – to believe that." He took my hand and squeezed. "Promise me, Cody."

"But –"

"No buts, son. Promise you'll remember."

A tiny bubble of blood appeared at the corner of his mouth. The creases in his face softened, almost like he was growing younger right before my eyes.

"I-I will," I said at last. "But I've got to go for help."

He shook his head. "You stay right here. That's all I

want. Just stay with me a spell."

Against my will I let him pull me down beside him until my forehead rested on his stubbly cheek. "Funny thing," he said, his arm around my shoulder. "Been out here hunting elk, and all I could think about was . . . buffalo. Strange, eh?"

"Don't talk," I pleaded. "You gotta lay still. Please, Dad." I buried my face against his shoulder. How could I tell Sam and Mom what happened? Would they hate me? I took a shuddering breath.

Would they ever speak to me again?

Dad stroked my rain-dampened hair. "Lord, I do wish you were older." His voice sounded weak, maybe even a little scared. "There's so much you need to know, so much that needs to be done to make it all happen."

The words came without thinking: "I-I'll just bring the herd home."

He gave me a puzzled look. "The herd . . . ?"

"Like Billy MacAllister," I said. "How he didn't quit after getting shot; he just sucked up the pain and followed the cattle. Rounded up those boys to help him. All he wanted was to bring the herd home. And he found a way." I lowered my eyes. *Even if he didn't live to see it.*

Dad smiled. "You've always had a good memory, Cody," he said, "So you just remember that too and I know everything will be all right."

I lay my head against his chest and closed my eyes.

He smelled like he always did: Old Spice and leather and campfire smoke.

"Lord, I do love you," he said, his voice soft as my winter quilt. "Never did say it quite . . . enough, I suppose. Hell, we never do. But you know it anyway, don't you? And you needn't fret, son. It don't really hurt."

Beyond the hotel doorway the sun climbed in the sky, spilling rays of light across the weed-choked street. Slowly I stood and walked outside where Zack waited patiently in the cool morning air. A patch of scraggly dandelions caught my eye. I bent and plucked one, twirling the pale yellow flower between my fingers.

In a million years, I would never have dreamed that Billy and my father had died right here in this place, separated by a century but linked somehow by those four little words. I supposed that each of them was only comforting someone they loved, but from Dad there was more than just that. To me those were words of forgiveness and maybe, words of hope, too.

Slowly I crushed the dandelion between my fingers, thinking about the promises I'd made that day, the ones I still hadn't kept. But there would be time for that later. Right this minute all I knew for sure was that the man I loved and the cowboy I'd been had ended their journeys here. Was mine about to begin? I guess it depended on how much of all this I wanted to believe, or as Angel might say, on how big a chance I wanted to take.

From somewhere nearby I heard the metallic buzz of motorbikes and the shouts of voices. Mounting up, I turned my back on the past – *my* past – and headed toward the sound.

The day after I returned we started work to fix up old Furnace Creek. Fortunately the old logging road where I heard the bikers made access pretty easy so it took only four more days to finish the job. We managed to do it all using just the materials we had on hand, too.

With construction done, Angel and I hung around to watch the actual filming. It was like nothing I'd ever seen; cameras and crew, lights, horses, extras – including Sam – and lots and lots of action. But cool as it all was I decided to skip the final scene; I couldn't bear watching Billy die again, even if it was only make believe.

Shooting wrapped yesterday. Liebowitz, J.T., cast and crew were already packed and gone. Today meant *adios* to Angel and her uncles. I knew it had to come eventually but I'd been dreading it since the first day we met.

The two of us spent the morning just wandering along the banks of Showerstall Creek, talking about pretty much everything but us. It felt kind of awkward. In a way we seemed to be pulling back from each other before saying goodbye. But as Angel reminded me, there really wasn't room to raise buffalo in Los Angeles. And I had to admit that Furnace Creek might not be the ideal spot for a custom furniture store either.

Those were our excuses but I think we both knew we had places to be and reasons to be there, and nothing we wanted or cared about was going to change that. Still, I hated the thought that one day Angel Suarez would just be somebody I used to know.

The afternoon air was hot and still as we sat by the creek, dangling our bare feet in the cool water. Finally Angel said "Okay, I gotta know before I leave; just how did your name get up on that ceiling?"

I smiled. "Took me a while but I finally remembered that too," I said. "Once we set up camp that day I decided I wanted to carve my name on something. See, I had this sweet new Buck knife I got for my birthday and –"

"Just like a guy," she said, punching my shoulder. "Always got to make your mark, right?"

"Anyway," I continued, "I talked Dad into letting me stand on his shoulders so I could carve it up high where everyone could see."

Angel rested her head against my arm and played with a lock of my hair; I was really going to miss that. "Funny how it all worked out, isn't it?" she asked.

"What do you mean?"

"Well, did you ever wonder if the twelve-year-old Cody left that message there just for you to find?"

Actually I'd been thinking about that too. If I hadn't chanced to see my name on the ceiling I might never have made the connection with my past.

"Could be, Angel," I said, "but I guess that's the one thing I'll never really know for sure."

A horn honked beyond the trees. After pulling on our sneakers we brushed the dirt from each other's jeans and walked back through the forest, holding hands for what would probably be the last time. As we passed the patch of gravel where the shower once stood, I remembered Angel in her faded robe, like a goddess with fiery hair. Had I really been afraid to ask her out that day? It seemed impossible to believe, like that had been some other kid, not me. I squeezed her hand and she tightened her fingers around mine.

Some other kid. In a way, I guessed it was.

Jimmy joined us while Angel stowed her gear in the pickup. He said nothing but gripped my shoulder and pumped my hand a few times before walking back to the panel truck where Bob and Luis waited.

She draped an arm around my neck. "Guess you're permanently off Jimmy's shit list, huh?"

I smiled weakly. "I reckon so."

"Then reckon *this.*" She pulled me into a rib-popping hug that almost lifted me off my feet and then slid into the cab of the pickup. My stomach knotted as I closed the door. I knew saying goodbye was going to hurt; I just didn't think it would hurt this much.

Angel pulled on a pair of wraparound sunglasses then laid her hands on the steering wheel, fingers drumming like always. "Cody, if there hadn't been a fire that day, do you . . . do you think we would have made love?"

Regretfully I shook my head.

She looked surprised. "Didn't you want to?"

"Oh hell yes!" I said quickly, putting my hand on her arm. "More than anything. But I thought it was just going to be another work day so I didn't come, you know, *prepared.*"

Angel pulled a foil wrapped condom from her shirt pocket. "I did."

Sunlight fell across the silvery surface, on the picture of a couple strolling barefoot on a sunlit beach. I remembered Angel's body warm and close against mine and the thought of us lying naked in the tent almost made my knees weak.

"Jesus," I said, glancing around, "where'd you get that?"

"Stole it from my brother's room." She twisted the thin package between her fingers. "Not that I was planning on anything at the time but I figured, what the hell, you never know."

My cheeks grew warm. "Angel . . ."

"Here." She pressed the condom into my hand and closed my fingers around it. "Won't be needing this with Jimmy keeping an eye on me again. Hell, I'll be lucky to have sex before I'm fifty."

"So you mean you haven't . . . that is, you're still –"

"A virgin? Yeah." She grinned. "Does it make any difference to ya, cowboy?"

We both said 'I love you' one last time then I leaned through the open window and gave her a kiss that I never wanted to end. Angel ran her fingers across my cheek and through my hair then gently pushed me away. Without looking back she popped the clutch and headed down the gravel road, around the bend and out of sight.

I sat on the hood of my truck till long after the dust had settled. Out of all the things that happened this summer, I'd never forget how it felt to fall in love with a girl who'd fallen in love with me.

The sun hung low in the sky when I turned into our driveway, surprised to see our old gray Lumina in the garage. Mom had called us just about every other day this

summer so I expected she'd let us know when she was on
her way home. It didn't matter; I took the porch steps two
at a time and burst through the front door.

In the kitchen Sam sat at the table eating a bowl of
ice cream while Mom stood at the sink washing dishes.
She smiled when she saw me and I put my arms around
her and hugged. After being on my own all summer it sure
felt wonderful to be somebody's kid again.

I raised an eyebrow at Sam but she shrugged and
mouthed 'I didn't know either.'

"Missed you, sweetheart," Mom said. "So how have
you been? Anything new?"

For days I'd been wondering and worrying how to
answer that question. Although I knew she would ask it
seemed impossible to explain everything I'd been through
this summer. Now I was just going to have to wing it.

Gently I pulled out the chair and had Mom sit down
next to Sam. Then I sat across the table from them and
folded my hands in front of me. "I think it's about time
we all talked," I said quietly.

Since I wasn't sure how – or where – to begin, I just
started with my first glimpse of buffalo clouds on that
gray, rainy day that seemed like a lifetime ago. Then as
other things came to me I wove them all into a story that
was part dreams, part reality and part who-knows-what.
Listening to myself I realized it sounded a little crazy and
I wondered if Sam and Mom thought I was making it all

up. But there was no head shaking or eye rolling from either of them, only silence till I mentioned seeing Tonka in the garage.

Sam slapped her hand on the table. "Ha! See, I *knew* he was yours!" she said, grinning. Mom gently shushed her then nodded for me to continue.

At last I got to our hunting trip. When I told them what really happened that day it almost killed me to watch their faces cloud with pain and hurt and loss. But I'd made up my mind to tell everything that happened, no matter what.

The words came faster and faster till I could hardly catch my breath. Finally I slumped back in the chair, completely exhausted. The room was so quiet I could hear drops of water splash into the sink full of dishes. The kitchen clock said almost two hours had passed since we sat down. I took a deep breath and braced myself for whatever would come next.

Mom reached across the table and took my hand. "Your father loved those hunting trips of yours," she said, looking into my eyes. "He'd do nothing but talk about them over and over for weeks after you two got back. What you did, where you went, what you saw, so in a way I got to live it too. Now he loved all of us of course, but that time he spent with you was really special to him."

My vision grew blurry and I lay my head on my arms,

fighting the urge to cry.

"I guess what I'm trying to say, Cody," she continued, "is that no matter what happened that day – or how, or why – I know there's no place on earth he'd rather have been than out there with you."

Tears came and this time I couldn't stop them. But then I heard the scrape of chairs and felt arms circle my shoulders, holding me tight.

"I miss him," Mom said, close to my ear. "Every single day."

"Me too," said Sam, her voice thick.

"He was my best friend. And when we lost him, well, for the longest time I wondered if the hurt would ever go away. But bad as that was, almost losing you was even worse. It was like you'd gone somewhere and shut the rest of us out. I never dreamed what you'd been carrying with you all these years, but I think it's time you put it down and come on back to the rest of us."

Sam gently kissed the back of my neck. "Yeah," she said. "Welcome home, Cody."

Later, when the house was dark and quiet I sat alone on the front porch swing and listened to the howl of coyotes in the distant hills. I glanced down at my hand; light from the living room window fell across a pale, jagged line on my palm. When I was ten I ripped it open on a barbed wire fence. I managed not to blubber as Dad washed the cut with his canteen but then he took my skin between his thumb and forefinger and squeezed. I cried out as blood welled up and dripped down my fingers.

Dad put a hand on my shoulder. "I know it hurts," he said softly, "but it cleanses the wound, son. Best way there is to make it heal."

Slowly I ran my finger down the thin white scar.

Ben Liebowitz called the next day to tell me Mr. Carlson had been paid, so at least I didn't have that to worry about. And once school started I pretty much forgot about everything until the film was scheduled to premiere at our Azatlan Theater on the day after Halloween. Since the summer all those memories of Billy MacAllister were fading. I didn't really want them stirred up again but I knew I had to go if for only one reason.

That night the theater was packed with what seemed like everyone in town. They cheered and booed in all the right places as the story unfolded. I sat between Mom and Sam but for me the movie passed in a blur till it reached the final showdown. Last summer before they shot that scene I took Ben aside and suggested just a slight change in the script, something I thought might sound better.

He smiled and said "maybe we'll give that a try."

And so up there on the screen, as Billy lay dying in the street he looked at the girl beside him and said the four words I knew were truly his last.

After the final credits – which included my name as 'Location Assistant' – I stood in the street while Ben accepted congratulations from people leaving the theater. As the crowd thinned out, Carrie Jackson and her posse strolled up to me.

"I thought that was really amazing, Cody," she said. "We all did. I had no idea that's what you were doing all summer." She smiled and touched my arm. "It must have been exciting. I'd really like to hear more about it sometime."

I smiled back. Lately, Carrie had gotten a whole lot more friendly; maybe I'd finally learned how to talk to a girl after all. "Well, how about this Wednesday?" I asked. "It's Family Night over at the Painted Lizard."

"I'd love to," she said, "but my folks are out so I've got to watch Tommy."

That was her younger brother. "No problem. Just bring him along and I'll drag my sister. They can hang out together. She's got quite a crush on him, you know."

"Really?" Carrie laughed. "And I think he likes Sam a lot too. Should we tell them?"

I shook my head. "Sam would kill me. Besides, maybe it would be better if they figured it out for themselves. It's more fun that way."

"Sounds like a plan," she said. "Guess I'll see you tomorrow in biology."

"Count on it." I replied. "Maybe we can, you know, dissect a frog together."

The posse giggled, but as they walked away Carrie

kept glancing back over her shoulder at me. Grinning, I waved and she waved back; it looked like biology was about to become my favorite subject.

When the street was finally empty Ben loosened his tie and lit a fresh cigar. "And that," he said with a huge grin, "is what we call show business, kid."

I couldn't help grinning back. "Gotta admit it was pretty amazing, Ben," I said. "Everyone seemed to love it. Real shame J.T. couldn't be here."

"Oh, don't feel too bad for him. Australia's pretty nice this time of year and you just don't pass up a role like the one he landed. I hear he got himself a pretty good advance, too."

"Lucky him."

He put a hand on my shoulder. "Now don't you worry, that point of yours is going pay off big time, I promise you. We generated a lot of positive buzz at the Telluride Film Festival last month. They're practically fighting over the foreign distribution rights so we're dubbing it into Spanish and German. Who knows, maybe even Japanese." He exhaled a satisfied cloud of smoke. "This is the chance I've been waiting for. All my goddamn life."

The night air was cool and I blew on my hands to warm them. "Congratulations," I mumbled.

"Of course," he added, "it may take a couple of years for you to get your full payback, unless . . ."

My ears perked up. "Unless what?"

Ben parked the cigar in the corner of his mouth and pulled an envelope from his pocket. "Okay, this is a once in a lifetime, take-it-or-leave-it offer," he said, waving it in front of my nose. "If you want to sell your point, I'll buy it back right now for –"

"Twenty thousand," I said quickly, grabbing a number out of thin air.

He raised an eyebrow. "Would you take thirty?"

"Uh, sure," I said, unsure at first if I'd heard him right. "That would be . . . great."

"Deal," he said and we shook on it. "You made yourself a real good choice there, kid."

I stared at the folded envelope. "Hope you don't mind me asking, Ben, but isn't a counter offer supposed to be for less, not more?"

"Usually, but this is a special case."

"Meaning . . . ?"

"Maybe we need to start at the beginning." Ben folded his arms. "See, offering you the point was J.T.'s idea. He told me so when we drove back to town from that corral. Said he figured you deserved a lot more than a few hundred bucks for teaching him how to ride."

"He did?"

"How about that? Knowing him, I thought it was pretty funny too, but I guess maybe you taught him some things besides just handling a horse. Anyway, he said you

two talked about a lot on that little overnighter of yours."
He scratched the side of his head. "Something about you
wanting to raise –"

"Buffalo."

He nodded. "And how some extra money might help
make a difference. But to get you to take the point he had
me plead poverty."

"He had you lie, you mean."

Ben winked. "We call it acting."

"So then you always had the money?"

"Not on your life. Not after the fire, anyway. If you
hadn't been lucky enough run across that old town up
there in the hills I'd probably be floating under Santa
Monica Pier about now." He grinned. "Face down."

Luck had nothing to do with me finding old Furnace
Creek but maybe that would stay my secret. I leaned
against the side of his Caddy. "I-I guess I don't know what
to say, Ben. No one's ever done anything like this for me."

"I'm just the middleman. The point came straight
from J.T.'s share." He paused by the door. "Say, what was
that girl's name?" he asked. "You remember, the Gallegos'
niece?"

"Angel," I said. "Angel Suarez." It almost sounded
strange saying her name out loud. Truth was, I hadn't even
thought about Angel for quite a while. But what was the
point? Although I really had loved her I was also pretty

sure we'd never see each other again.

"That's her. She stopped by my office before I left and gave me something to bring you."

Inside the trunk was a flat wooden crate so big it took both of us to lug it to my truck. When we were done Ben slid behind the Caddy's wheel. "She said you'd probably know where to open it." He held up a paper bag. "But this might help if you don't."

"Thanks," I said as he handed it over. "Thanks for everything, Ben."

He put the car in gear. "Kid," he said, "when did I ever do anything for you?"

I watched him drive away before I opened the bag. Inside was a package of vanilla wafers and a Hershey bar.

Cookies and chocolate.

A half hour later I reached that mountain valley ringed with towering, silent cliffs. I drove slowly down and parked at the edge of the pond, which was steaming slightly in the night air. Winter was coming on and the night sky stretched cold and starry overhead with just a sliver of a white, crescent moon. I opened the package and ate a cookie, then another, looking out across the darkened meadow.

Dad had been wrong about our family raising buffalo. Although this valley really was the perfect place when I actually ran the numbers it didn't make sense for us, at least not on our own. Had we done it his way we'd be in even worse financial shape than before. Once I would probably have just given up, but not after remembering the promises I'd made to Dad, and more important, to myself.

And so last month I organized a meeting with some of the other ranchers who were in the same fix as us and proposed that if everyone banded together, maybe we could all make a go of it.

I was pretty surprised they would even listen to a kid like me, let alone agree, but the papers for the new Furnace Creek Bison Association sat on our kitchen table, drawn up and ready to go. The only signature missing was mine. Mom could have signed but since I'd just turned eighteen she said it was now up to me.

"Your father would have wanted it that way," she told me.

That was probably true, and while the extra money would sure help, were we – was *I* – really ready for this? I picked up a tire iron and walked to the back of the truck, wishing I knew whether this was truly the right choice to make.

After a couple of minutes work the crate popped open and I flicked on my flashlight to see what it was.

"Well I'll be damned," I whispered.

Inside the crate lay a large wooden sign and on its surface the carved image of a buffalo. Hairy curls covered its massive body, broken only by horns and hooves and a single eye painted in shining gold. Across the top of the sign ran the words 'T BAR S RANCH' in large block letters. Below it simply read 'The Harrisons' in a delicate flowing script. No note, just this sign.

I felt along the edges till I found a string of letters carved on the bottom: **A. Suarez**. Closing my eyes I pictured Angel working on it, long hours with a hammer and chisel in those talented hands of hers. Wood shavings nestled like snowflakes in her hair. Sawdust clung to her cheeks, her lips . . . *and if I kissed her, she'd probably taste like it too.*

The silent buffalo stared up at me with its golden eye as if asking: *so what now, Cody?* Slowly I traced the words on the sign, my finger following the smooth deep grooves. It really was beautiful; it would be a real shame to let something like this go to waste.

I bit off a corner of the Hershey bar and let it melt on my tongue before sliding the lid back in place. On the ground a smooth white pebble caught my eye. I picked it up, felt its cold weight in the palm of my hand and flung it far out over the pond. It splashed unseen in the darkness.

"Thanks, Angel," I said softly. *For everything.*

As if in answer, rings of moonlight rippled across the water till they lapped the shore at my feet.

ABOUT THE AUTHOR

CRAIG SANDERS has long been fascinated by the West. A native of Indiana, he grew up in Ohio and moved to Colorado to attend Colorado State University. He has worked as a cook, park ranger, census taker, railroader, laborer, fence-builder, and health inspector.

He has three children and six grandchildren and lives with his wife Deborah in Lakewood, Colorado.

www.ingramcontent.com/pod-product-compliance
Lightning Source LLC
Chambersburg PA
CBHW021032130626
46552CB00005B/1797